Compelled to Love a Stranger

By Teri Sharbaugh

Compelled To Love a Stranger
by Teri Sharbaugh

Printed in the United States of America

ISBN 978-1-60647-155-5

www.xulonpress.com

I dedicate this book to my husband, Norm, who has made our lives together a fascinating excursion instead of a tedious trek.

CHAPTER 1

As Katie unlocked the door to her small apartment, her mind was agitated with a multitude of thoughts. She hadn't realized until recently how uneventful the first twenty years of her life had been. She'd grown up reasonably happy with her mom and dad and her brother, Mark, who was three years younger than she. After high school a two-year secretarial course had launched her into a great job for a girl fresh out of business school. She had hoped to find that perfect husband and live happily ever after. That was before the accident.

Even though that fateful day had occurred two years ago, she could remember it as if it were yesterday. She had been unpacking the last of her belongings, carefully deciding where each of her private treasures should go in her tiny, newly rented apartment. The phone had jingled merrily, but when she had lifted the receiver she heard Mark's frantic voice. At the mention of the word "police" she had thought maybe Mark had gotten himself in some sort of trouble, but as she had pieced together his disjointed words, she had realized the police were there to report an accident. In simple terms, her parents were both dead, killed instantly in a head-on collision. In those moments it had seemed that her world stood still, and when it started up again she was headed in an entirely different direction.

She had moved back home with Mark for a while, but when the estate was settled it was clear that the insurance wasn't enough to pay off the mortgage, so she couldn't afford to keep the house. Everything had been sold and that money along with the moderate insurance money had been deposited safely in the bank. That detail had been the only positive aspect of the whole nightmare. The insurance money would give Mark the opportunity to go straight to college. He wouldn't have to stay out a couple of years to earn the money. If they were very careful, he should have enough to cover his total college expenses.

Once Mark had moved on campus, life had seemed to go back to some form of normalcy.

As far as she had been able to tell, he was smoothly adjusting to college life and making friends. Even his grades that first year were more than acceptable. Katie had thought everything was going to turn out all right after all, as impossible as that had seemed in those dark days just after the accident.

Then, during that second year after the tragedy, Katie had begun to notice that she didn't hear from Mark as often as she had in the beginning. She had decided that he had to make his own life and maybe they were just growing apart. Surely it was just natural.

The next worry had come with the last quarterly bank statement for their joint savings account. There had been two significant withdrawals. Mark's explanation was that he had made early payments on his school bill to guarantee he could get the classes he wanted. Katie hadn't argued with him, but she had felt uneasy. Somehow his story just hadn't rung true, but Mark had never lied to her before. At least as far as she knew, he hadn't.

Then her latest concern had come only last week. Mark had staggered to her door about one o'clock in the morning. He had been severely beaten. A trip to the emergency room had revealed a broken jaw, three cracked ribs, a couple of teeth out, and a dislocated elbow. He had told the police that he was jumped by two masked assailants while going from his dorm to his car. According to Mark they tried to rob him, then became angry and began to beat him when he only had three dollars in his billfold. There weren't any witnesses to the attack and even Mark hadn't seen their faces. Katie was extremely concerned about Mark, but what could she do? He was almost twenty years old and she wasn't his mother.

Now as she changed into casual clothes and started another dinner for one, she couldn't get over the uneasy feeling that all was not well. Totally absorbed by her thoughts, she was startled by an aggressive knock. Opening the door tentatively, she observed a well-dressed man probably in his late fifties. Before she had time to consider whether she would open the door further, he had managed to stealthily slip past her and close the door behind him.

"Sorry, Miss, to intrude this way, but we have some pressing business to discuss," the stranger's words came with a touch of urgency.

Katie's mind raced to find a way to call for help. The telephone was close, but so was the man. If she screamed, would anyone hear? Or would she just be embarrassed to find this was the new manager of the apartment complex? As fear mounted on the inside, she strained to maintain enough control to listen to what the man was saying.

"I was much distraught to hear of your brother's misfortune last week," continued the calm measured tone. "What is this world coming to when a young man isn't safe walking to his car at night?"

At this point Katie wondered if it might be proper for her to make some polite comment, but her fear was so great not one word came to her mind. Something deep within told her that this man had something to do with Mark's beating. But he certainly didn't match the description of the young hoodlums that her brother had reported to the police.

In desperation, she moved slightly toward the small white telephone that sat on the lamp table only two feet away.

"Miss Montgomery, I really wish you would be so kind as to postpone any telephone calls until after we have had our talk," cautioned the intruder in a polite but menacing tone.

Katie found her voice enough to mumble, "What is it you've come to talk about?"

"I assume you are not aware that your brother, Mark Montgomery, owes a substantial sum of money to my employer. He has neglected his payments of late, for which a reminder was given last week. Mark made a withdrawal from your joint savings account, but it was not sufficient to satisfy his debt. Since your brother was reticent to share his dilemma with you, his only relative, my employer thought it only fair to enlighten you as to the details of his present circumstance."

Now Katie's fear was evolving to confusion and well on its way to anger. She asked very deliberately, "Just why does Mark owe you this large amount of money?"

"Not me, Miss — my employer — who wishes to remain anonymous and has therefore sent me to have this conversation with you. But to answer your question, I'm afraid your brother has been doing a bit of gambling after school. And I might add, he's not very good at it."

Gambling! Never in her wildest dreams had she imagined this possibility. Why? How? When did all this start? But in these moments of silence all the pieces were fitting together. Mark's seeming distance and coolness, the savings account withdrawal, the beating …

The fear was back. "Just how much trouble is my brother in? How much money does he owe?" Katie managed.

"Well, Miss Montgomery, I believe the total is just over $25,000. My employer is extending his credit until May 5th. That gives him three more weeks, which considering the fact that this was due to be paid in full by March 12th is very generous of my employer, you'll have to admit."

Katie wasn't prepared to admit anything of the sort at this point, but she had to ask another question, even though she really didn't want to know the answer.

"Excuse me, Mr. ...?"

"Joe, Miss Montgomery. Call me Joe."

"Well, Joe..." Katie paused for several moments, took a deep breath and plunged on. "Joe, just what happens if Mark is unable to make this payment on time. You see we have no close relatives or friends with that kind of money readily available. Considering our ages and the fact that we have no collateral, I can't imagine any bank giving us a loan for that amount. What happens if we can't come up with the money?" Her voice trembled slightly making her inner turmoil quite apparent.

Joe didn't respond immediately, weighing his answer carefully. When he finally spoke she could almost detect some emotion in his voice.

"Now, Miss, I'm going to be straight with you. I can see you're a good kid. I'd really like to give you a break, but it isn't up to me. I'm just here to give you the message — to tell you I'll be back to collect the full amount on May 5th. You understand now it isn't me. It's my employer. But because I like you, I gotta warn you. You want to be sure you've got that money come May. I can't be responsible for what happens if I come to collect and you don't have the cash. One more thing: don't get any crazy ideas about disappearing. My employer has ways to find people, you understand. But now don't worry. I can tell you're a smart one. You'll figure something out. I feel sure of that."

"But Mr.…I mean Joe, you still haven't told me what will happen." Katie was losing composure and her voice showed it.

That told Joe it was time for him to leave. He'd done his job.

"Well, Miss Montgomery, it's not for me to say exactly. But like I said, you just have that money right here on May 5th. Of course, you understand not to involve any law in this. That really wouldn't be healthy. Just get that money. You're a smart one. You can do it."

With that he slipped out the door as quickly as he had slipped in a few minutes before. He really wasn't as sure as he sounded that she could come up with the cash, and he actually felt badly about it.

"Joe, you must be getting soft, or maybe you're getting too old for this kind of work," he mumbled to himself as he walked to the car. "Or maybe this kid's getting to you because she reminds you of your sister's kid, Dorie. She always was your favorite, and now with her getting married next week… Oh, well, it's out of my hands. I'm just doing my job. Maybe the kid'll come through after all, and the whole affair won't have to get nasty," he comforted his slightly-ruffled conscience. Then, putting his car in gear, he hurried home to get ready for his trip to Chicago to see his favorite niece tie the knot.

CHAPTER 2

Lucas knew this was a bad idea. Why was he at this stupid wedding anyway? He barely knew Dan, Jr., but old Mr. Barnes had made it extremely clear that Lucas was expected to be at his only son's wedding. And Lucas had determined he would use any and every means possible to land that upcoming promotion.

Yet, this kind of reminder of his past was exactly what Lucas had been trying to insulate himself from for the last three years. Right now his mind was out of control as he watched the bride walk down the aisle dressed in the flowing white gown. Did she look that much like Adrian walking down the same aisle seven years ago? Could it really have been that long? It seemed like just a couple of years. But then again, in some ways it seemed like an eternity.

His thoughts raced unrestrained to those early days. First he had graduated from college with a double major in business and communications. He couldn't believe his luck in landing the job of his dreams at a large flourishing family television network. As he was making his way up the ranks, he fell head over heels for a beautiful brunette. Adrian had everything. Cascades of wavy dark hair surrounded her large alluring eyes. Her figure was the envy of all the girls at the network. The most fantastic fact was that she fell for him, too. They seemed to click immediately and were married one year after their first date.

They moved into a pretentious house in the country with a few partly-wooded acres, snuggled up against a miniature forest preserve. It was a bit much for a couple of newly-weds, but with two good salaries they had enough to live quite comfortably.

As the months went by, their passion for each other cooled some, but Lucas assumed this was something all couples experience. Then several months into their third year, he had begun to worry. Adrian was as attractive as ever, but she seemed dissatisfied with their "storybook" existence. She talked about not being fulfilled. Lucas suggested they start a family, but instead Adrian was thinking about going back to school to continue her education. She wanted to accomplish something of value with her life. She also slipped in a suggestion that after almost three years without a pregnancy, maybe they wouldn't be able to have children.

From that time on, things went downhill. She quit her well-paying job and started school fulltime, placing a definite strain on their budget as well as their relationship. In public they were still the perfect couple, but at home Adrian had grown distant, finding more and more reasons to be away. Lucas wasn't ready to give up on his marriage. He wanted to return to what they had that first year so he had begun to court and woo his beautiful wife again.

Lucas had been sure his plan was working. In spite of the financial strain, they planned a second honeymoon in Hawaii. Two weeks before their romantic getaway, Adrian had left to spend the weekend at her sister's home in Michigan about two hours away. The next morning, Lucas had been lazily reading the paper and drinking a cup of coffee when the call came. It was Adrian's sister. Adrian had been seriously injured in an accident and was in the hospital. Could he please hurry? But no amount of rushing would help Lucas.

Adrian was dead within minutes of that phone call. When he finally reached the hospital, the news was more agonizing than anything he could imagine. As he spoke with Adrian's sister, he became aware of the fact that Adrian had not been alone in the car. She and another man were pulling out of the parking lot of the motel where they had spent the night together when they were hit by another vehicle. Once Lucas found out that the affair with a fellow student had been going on for several months, he shut himself off. He didn't want to know any more. He was grief stricken and full of fury and intense hatred all at once.

Because the accident was out of state, Lucas managed to keep the sordid affair a secret. Everyone was full of sympathy, encouraging Lucas to take a few weeks off to pull himself together before returning to work. What a horrible shame it was to see such a perfect couple torn apart prematurely. On and on the office talk had gone.

The time at home spent alone was probably the worst thing Lucas could have done. He had spent hours on end scrutinizing the last few months of memories, looking for clues that he should have seen which foreshadowed his wife's unfaithfulness. So many things had begun to make sense. She had insisted on moving into the other bedroom. She said she needed more room for her clothes, and she'd be able to stay up and study late without bothering him. When the nights they spent together became fewer, Lucas just assumed she was overwhelmed with schoolwork. Yet the one small clue that nearly pushed him over the edge was a bottle of men's cologne. He had found it on the sink of Adrian's private bathroom. It was almost empty, but it was a scent he had never used. As he had realized whom it had belonged to and what its presence in his wife's room meant, he had felt utterly stupid. Surely he should have seen it. Had they laughed at his naiveté? This thought had filled him with a white hot fury. As he had felt it wash over him, Lucas had allowed a deep bitterness to move in to protect him from any further pain. He just couldn't take any more. A blessed numbness had taken the place of his grief, but the bitterness never subsided.

After a while he had gone back to work and appeared to be doing fine. He could still be friendly, even charming, but he felt cold and dead inside. As first one year then another went by, his bitterness toward Adrian was redirected to women in general. Sometime during the last year, he had begun spinning a fantasy in his mind. Two factors contributed to his bitter musings. First there was the endless problem of keeping an acceptable housekeeper. He fired a few because they were inept, but most quit after only a few weeks. He could only maintain his likeable demeanor as long as he was at the office. It was too difficult to pretend all the time, so he took out all his frustrations on the woman who was doing what his own wife should have been doing. If only…

Then there was the pressure Lucas was getting from the boss, Old Man Barnes. He really wanted that new position that was opening up. The way Lucas viewed it, Mr. Wilbur D. Barnes was an antiquated fool. The old codger thought that since they were representing a family network, this sort of high position should be held by someone who was married, who had a family. And the bottom line was that Mr. Barnes' influence would pretty much determine who would fill that position. He had been patient with Lucas. It had been over three years since Adrian died, but now he was throwing out obvious hints about Lucas marrying again. It was all too apparent that his advancement at the network may well rest on whether Lucas moved toward that goal.

As Lucas had pondered all this in his bed alone every night, he had come up with the perfect solution … perfect, but impossible. What he needed was an old fashioned bondservant. For a sum of money he could buy someone's freedom. She would in turn become his wife, clean his house, cook his meals, even satisfy his physical desires — but all this without the emotional ties. He would never again leave himself open for such pain and humiliation as he had suffered with Adrian. He would never again trust a woman. Maybe there were a few good ones out there, but the price of taking a chance was too high. He would never again put himself in that position.

The only problem with his far-fetched fantasy was that the whole idea was entirely preposterous. The day of the bondservant was over, yet somehow dreaming up details to his fantasy entertained him on those lonely nights. It seemed to relieve the bitterness ... or maybe it only nursed it.

Now here he sat at this wedding reliving past days he didn't want to recall. At least the ceremony was over. He'd make his appearance at the reception, have a few drinks, then slip away from these horrible reminders.

A couple of drinks later, he found himself seated by the bride's uncle. Once the alcohol had begun to sooth his pains of reminiscence, he began to open up to this likeable, middle-aged man. They exchanged a few cynical jokes about wedded bliss. About then, Mr. Barnes stopped by to thank him for coming to his son's wedding. As usual there was the hint bordering on a threat. He was hoping Lucas was looking for a wife to help him climb the ladder at WJMB.

A few more drinks on an empty stomach loosened Lucas' tongue more than he dreamed possible. The wedding had surfaced old wounds, and this fellow seemed to draw the words out of him. Before he realized what he was saying, he had spilled out his whole impossible fantasy to a perfect stranger. Oh well, after today he'd probably never see this man again. And there was no law against imagining such things.

Joe had been quite content to listen to Lucas' babbling. Actually, Joe's twenty year experience with a nagging wife was enough to make the impossible fantasy attractive even to him. He couldn't help but notice the discomfort which Mr. Barnes' obvious hints had brought to his new acquaintance.

Then it came to him. Maybe there was a one-in-a-million chance this troubled man could bring his wild fantasy to life. And it would make a messy job much easier for him as well. That pretty Montgomery kid had crossed his mind as he saw Dorie walk down the aisle so vivacious and happy. Just for a moment, he'd pictured the frightened face in contrast. He'd told himself he was a crazy old coot for letting her get to him, but maybe this crazy old coot could help solve everybody's problems. He couldn't reveal his ideas in such a public place. A bit of privacy was in order.

"Lucas, my boy, I might just have a solution to your problem. Will you join me at a favorite club of mine in a couple of hours? It's only a few blocks away from here. My dear wife will surely be spending the entire evening with her sister after the bride and groom's departure. Meet me there at about seven tonight. If you'd like to hear my proposition, that is."

And, with that invitation, the two men parted company — the older to ponder the possibilities and the younger to stew in curiosity.

CHAPTER 3

As Lucas entered the dimly lit room of Joe's club, he asked himself again why he had agreed to this meeting. He had no idea what kind of proposition the man was talking about, and he barely knew this Joe. But the truth was that the last place he wanted to go now was to that lonely house in the country to relive the past seven years in his already agitated mind. He might as well relieve his curiosity and distract himself a little longer. He'd already exposed his deepest, darkest longings to this stranger. He might as well see what he had to say.

After welcoming Lucas to a corner booth, Joe wasted little time on preliminaries. Lucas could tell that the older man was trying to suppress his excitement.

"You know, Lucas, the more I think about my little plan, the more I think it might be insane enough to work. Except for one thing, that is. I'm wondering if you can afford my little enterprise."

Lucas wasn't yet prepared to reveal his financial status to his new friend, but whatever Joe was getting at, finances were the least of his concerns. Mortgage insurance had paid off their mammoth house at Adrian's death. And the insurance settlement for the accident had been unbelievable. With a lucrative job and no one to buy for, Lucas had more money than he had ever dreamed of having at this stage of his life.

Though he wasn't ready to offer any information at this point, he was sure money was not a problem.

"Joe, why don't you just tell me what's on your mind? I really don't have the slightest idea what we're talking about," Lucas responded, starting to get impatient.

"Okay, my boy, but I'm not sure where to start." After a long pause, Joe plunged into a description of his scheme. "When you were sharing with me your … uh … what should I say … your 'impossible dream,' it sort of came to me that I might be able to help you out. You see; I recently made the acquaintance of a young lady in desperate need of a large sum of money … that is $35,000, to be exact. Now I'm thinking her need could be desperate enough that she might consider accepting the type of offer you were discussing at the wedding today. I don't know for sure, mind you. She might have come up with the money on her own by now, but I'm just thinking that if she hasn't yet, she just might be willing to listen."

As Joe paused to see the reaction of the younger man facing him, the only emotion he could read at first was disbelief. Then another look emerged. Distrust? Yes, there was definitely a look of distrust.

"Joe, you've got to be kidding. I was just babbling today. You didn't take me seriously, did you? What I was talking about was off the wall. You just can't go down to the corner market and buy a wife. And if you could … well, it sounds almost illegal! What kind of girl would agree to such a thing? She certainly would not be the kind of woman I'd want to bring into my home."

"Now, I couldn't be sure she'd agree, and we'd never know till we asked her; but I do know she's in serious trouble, and I'm just as sure she's a nice kid. I'm positive you two would get along just fine."

"Wait a minute! You said a nice kid. How old is this "kid" anyway?"

Joe thought a moment. "I'd say early twenties. Don't worry; she's not a minor."

After an uncomfortable pause, Lucas shot back a further question. "If she's so nice and so available, I'm guessing she must be somewhat "unattractive". Now be honest. Tell me what she looks like."

"Sounds to me like you're getting the least bit interested, so I really am going to be honest. She's not gorgeous. She's probably not the looker your first wife was, but she's real nice looking. She's about medium height and weight with brown hair and brown eyes. I guess that's as much as I can remember. But like I said she's a nice kid, and I'd like to see her get out of this jam. For that matter, I'd like to see you get what you want. I think we could all help each other."

"That brings up another point, Joe. What's in this for you?"

Seeing new suspicion in the other man's eyes, Joe quickly spoke up, "Not a thing, my boy. I just happened to be the one in the middle to hear both stories and see that it could be that you two were made for each other." Joe thought it best not to mention the $10,000 difference in the amount the girl needed and what he was asking from Lucas. If the boy had the money and Joe got what his employer wanted without any rough business, he figured he deserved a little commission for his trouble.

They sat in silence for several minutes. Joe figured his best option was to keep quiet and let all of this sink in. Just as he hoped, Lucas' mind was racing with the possibility. He knew it would never work out like his "impossible dream," but if it worked well enough to secure that promotion, it just might be worth it.

"What am I thinking!?" he silently exclaimed. "How can I actually be considering this crazy idea?"

Finally, after what seemed like an eternity to Joe, Lucas spoke up. "Joe, I have to admit that you've given me something to think about, but I can't just go along with this without first giving it some more serious consideration. How long will you be in town?"

"Sure, my boy, I understand. A thing like this … well, a fellow has to really chew on it a while to get things straight. I'll be around here a couple more days. The wife and I will probably head out of here Sunday night. Here's my number. Just give me a call and let me know what you decide. If you decide you're interested, I'll have to check on the other end … see if there's any chance she's interested, you know."

"Thanks, Joe," Lucas said quietly. "I'll get back with you."

As Lucas drove home that night, his thoughts went from disbelief and horror to excitement and anticipation. Before he reached home, he knew he was going to go for it. If he didn't, he'd spend the rest of his life wondering what would have happened if he'd taken this one in a million long shot. What was the worst that could happen? He'd find out it was a big mistake and get a quick divorce. It's not like he'd be heart broken. If it gave him his chance at that promotion, it would be worth the money. What would Adrian say if she knew he was spending a chunk of her insurance money to buy himself a wife? He laughed out loud just thinking about it. A cynical laugh maybe, but it was the first time he could remember actually laughing out loud since … well, since long before Adrian died.

Yet he couldn't just fall into this. He had to get organized. If he was going to do this crazy thing, he was going to do it right. Where should he begin? They would have to have some sort of agreement. He'd put it in writing. Lucas wished he knew some way to make her abide by this contract.

All Saturday he labored over "the agreement." It may not be legal, but he wanted this woman to understand exactly what she was getting into before she signed on the dotted line or said "I do." By Saturday night he was satisfied with his work and called Joe, giving him the go ahead to contact the woman and set up a meeting if she was interested. Then he'd lay all his cards on the table. If she said yes and he approved of what he saw, he would go ahead with it. What could he lose?

CHAPTER 4

As Katie walked through the door of her apartment, she felt like her brain was on fire. As soon as the strange man named Joe had left her several days ago, she had gone to work on her problem. She had contacted Mark and with him laid out a plan of action to somehow some way come up with $25,000 on short notice.

This afternoon she had tried the very last option on her list. It was hard to believe all the rejections she had received the last few days. She had tried so hard to express the desperation of her need without revealing the ugly details of their debt. *Their* debt? It was Mark's debt really, but she had felt such a responsibility for her younger brother when her parents passed away that she automatically assumed his foolish debt as her own. Besides, Joe had come to her. No doubt he had figured out that this young college student wasn't imaginative enough to solve his own financial problems. It was apparent that Joe's employer didn't care where the money came from as long as he was paid in full.

Personally, Katie didn't have that many close friends, and the few friends she had just plain didn't have that kind of money. In spite of that, she had received promises of help that amounted to about $2,000.

She looked into loans at many banks and even called about credit cards, but with absolutely no credit history, no financial institution was willing to take a chance on a young woman who just turned twenty three with no equity.

Mark had even less luck than his sister. He had been to his companions too many times before, asking to be bailed out of lesser problems of the same type. By now, his friends had learned to go the other way when they saw him coming. They felt that to give him any more would just encourage him to continue his gambling.

The young man had made an attempt to escape his problems. A short time ago he had joined the army. He had hoped this would get him out of harm's way before his foolishness had caught up with him, but the government had not moved quickly enough. Now his sister was involved, and he was almost paralyzed with fear.

Katie wasn't sure about this new development. She would be glad to have her brother away from the immediate danger, but she was sure he would face similar temptations in the armed forces, and she wouldn't be around to help.

Then again, what help had she been anyway. She was no closer to a solution than when she started. The hopelessness collapsed in around her like a dense fog. From deep within she let out a cry to God. She had thought recently how strange it was that when all else failed, she found herself calling on God. She hadn't bothered Him much in the past except when her parents had been killed. She promised Him then that if He would help her through that crisis, she would never ask anything of Him again, but here she was with nowhere else to go. She hoped God would understand and help her get out of this nightmare.

Physical and emotional exhaustion began to take its toll. She began to weep quietly in her lonely apartment. Finally she fell into a troubled sleep. She woke with a start, feeling confused and disoriented. Then she heard the sound that must have awakened her initially. There was a firm steady knock at the door. She froze as fear began to penetrate her grogginess. Another knock was followed by a familiar voice.

"Miss Montgomery, it's just me, Joe," the voice said cheerfully as if it belonged to an old family friend. "Could I come in for a few minutes and talk to you?"

Now some of Katie's fears were replaced by anger. "You said Mark had until May 5th to pay his debt. What are you doing here early?" she answered with more confidence than she felt.

"Oh no, Miss Montgomery, I'm not here to collect. Don't you be thinking anything like that. Joe's not here to collect today. Something's come up and I'm here with … well, I guess you'd say I'm here with a proposition. Please, let me come in and talk with you."

Joe couldn't remember the last time he'd said "please" to an individual from whom he was collecting. This girl was definitely getting under his skin. The sooner he got this taken care of the better.

Katie sat in silence pondering her choices. She had absolutely no hope of getting the money in time. Did she have any reason to refuse listening to this man?

As the door opened slowly, Joe looked down into large red-rimmed eyes. He could see she'd been crying. His heart went out to her. He really hoped this deal would work out for her. He'd have to choose his words carefully.

"Could I just sit down a minute, Miss?" Joe asked meekly.

Her answer was abrupt. "What's the proposition you brought?"

There was an awkward silence as Joe sat down uninvited. Katie didn't move. She was tired and upset. She had no intention of being polite to this intruder.

"Let me say first, Miss Montgomery, that I'm here on my own this evening … that is to say … I'm not representing my employer. To tell the truth, I was afraid a young lady like you would have trouble finding the $25,000 in the prescribed amount of time. So, when I met a gentleman at my sister's kid's wedding last Friday and we got to chatting friendly-like ... well, I got me an idea about how I could help you out."

Katie interrupted, "Could you just please make it short and tell me why you're here?"

"And that's just what I'm doing, Missy, if you'll just hear me out now."

With a sigh of resignation, Katie finally sat down across from the man.

"Miss Montgomery, last week I had the good fortune to make the acquaintance of a young man. I liked the fellow from the very first and after conversing with him for some time, I was made aware that my new friend had a problem that was causing him great concern."

"But, Joe, what could this possibly have to do with me?" Katie interrupted, still impatient.

"Just hear me out, Missy, and I'll get to that. As I was saying, my friend has a problem. He works for one of those family-type TV channels, and there is a position coming up that he wants real bad. But his employer is kind of an old fashioned sort and he thinks whoever gets this new position should be married."

"I can see you're starting to follow me. That's right. My friend isn't married, and he doesn't have any prospects."

Trying to ignore a sick feeling in the pit of her being, she whispered, "What's wrong with this man that he can't find a woman who would marry him?"

"Oh no, no, no! It's not like that, really," Joe soothed. "It's like this. You see, he had a wife, but she passed on some three years ago in a tragic automobile accident, I believe. And, well, he just never has found anyone else. You understand, don't you, Miss Montgomery?"

The words automobile accident struck a note of sympathy in Katie's jumbled thoughts. She surely knew how devastating that kind of loss could be. Yet even taking this into consideration, could this be legitimate?

"So you see, I thought with you needing so much money and my friend having plenty of money and in dire need of a wife ... well, I thought maybe you could help each other out."

When Joe paused for a moment, Katie asked, "Just what are you proposing?"

"Well, I'm so glad you asked," Joe began cheerily. "My friend put everything he expects down on paper. I'm going to leave this here for you to look over carefully. If you're interested at all, just call this number right here at the bottom and ask for Joe, and I'll set up a little meeting so you two can make each other's acquaintance and then make a decision. If you're not interested, don't you think I'll hold that against you at all. You've still got till May 5th, and I won't bother you at all until then."

With that, he handed her several sheets of neatly-typed paper and was gone before she said a word. For a while Katie just sat still, staring ... not reading any words ... just staring ... trying to comprehend what had just happened.

Finally she focused in and began to read. The whole thing looked very formal, almost like a legal document. It listed requirements for her as well as listing a few things the author assured her he would require of himself.

As she read through each line, she wasn't sure this made her feel better about this "proposition" or worse. The emotionless statements brought a chilling effect. First of all, she was expected to obey immediately and without question. For his part he agreed not to require anything unreasonable of her. Katie was thinking that what was "unreasonable" might be a matter of opinion.

As she continued down the page, she read that she would not be physically abused in any way. She would be provided for in every way, including the debt she presently owed. The thought went through her mind again at this point, that it was really her brother Mark's debt, not her own, but there was no point in thinking about that now.

One part she would have found almost comical if the whole situation wasn't so frightening: there was to be no unnecessary conversation. She wondered if he was afraid of getting stuck with a chatterbox who would bore him to death.

She read on. She would be expected to take care of cooking, housework, and laundry. This would have to be done in an organized fashion, including written weekly and monthly plans. As Katie stopped and pondered this one, her first reaction was distaste. Though she was very organized at the office, she had not put those skills to work at home. The more she thought about it, the better it sounded. She was sure it would be much better to prioritize housework. This would just make her get organized. It would probably be much better that way.

Katie suddenly realized she was beginning to consider this crazy deal. How could she even think about it? Then again, what choice did she have? Where else could she come up with $25,000, and what would happen to Mark if she didn't? She wished she knew more about this kind of thing.

"If only I had someone I could confide in who could advise me," she mumbled mournfully. Her troubled thoughts continued to bombard her mind. Would these people really do anything serious for that money? Yet that beating Mark took was very real. What if they actually ended up killing Mark? She couldn't take that chance. She'd never forgive herself. She'd better read the rest of this strange offer.

In a cool, formal tone, the next point made it clear that this would be a marriage of convenience, not a marriage of love, but it would be a real marriage. It would be consummated. How odd! It almost seemed like a warning not to get her hopes up that they would fall in love and live happily ever after. She was not to expect that.

The last paragraph explained that if, after a year, he was not satisfied with the arrangement, the marriage would be ended, and she would be given alimony until she remarried. This stirred up some old memories ... talks she had had with her mother. Her mother had made her promise that she would choose her husband carefully and make a commitment that would last a lifetime. She told her to take divorce out of her vocabulary and work to make her marriage last.

But her Mom never dreamed that her only daughter would be put in a predicament like this. What would she think? How would she advise her daughter?

Tears came to Katie's eyes. She missed her mother so much right now. She so wished she could run to her as a refuge. Surely Mom and Dad could have found some solution. But Katie had nowhere to run. There was no one to help. She was on her own and felt very small and weak and tired.

After she read the paper through three more times, she decided to call her brother. This was really his problem. He should be aware of what was going on with this proposition. Her first temptation had been to keep this a secret and somehow protect him from feeling the guilt he was bound to feel when he heard this plan. After further consideration, she decided Mark needed to understand the serious consequences of his gambling. Maybe it would be a deterrent to future problems, especially while he was away in the army. Mark joined Katie at her apartment within minutes of her call.

"This idea is outrageous!" Mark exploded when he heard the plan. "Whoever suggested this should be horsewhipped!

The whole idea is absurd! No way am I going to let you go through with this!"

Katie interrupted quietly. "And what are you going to do about it? Can you come up with $25,000 by May 5th?"

"Sis, you can't be thinking about agreeing to this insanity. I'd never forgive myself. There has to be another way," Mark retorted.

"There may be, but we've got to face the fact that we have yet to find it. And I don't have anything left to try. Do you?"

Mark just stood there looking miserable. After a long silence, Katie started talking again in a quiet voice. "I'm going to call Joe and set up a meeting. I'll just have to wait until I meet this man to make a final decision. You keep trying to get the $25,000. If you come up with any possibilities at all, you let me know right away."

When Katie looked up at her brother, she saw tears in his eyes. Now his voice was soft and husky as he said, "I'm so sorry, Sis. So very, very sorry."

CHAPTER 5

The meeting was set up for 7:00 P.M. the next Saturday at Katie's apartment. Lucas had requested they meet at her apartment. He thought it would give him a better idea of her character by seeing how she lived, decorated, and kept her place up. He thought things were going smoother than he had imagined possible, but he was ready to put on the brakes if he didn't like what he saw at the introduction. His anticipation heightened as the day and hour grew closer. He was to fly out Saturday afternoon. Joe would meet him at the airport and take him to the apartment.

Katie, on the other hand, was feeling a turmoil of conflicting emotions. The thought that she might meet the man she would marry both exhilarated and terrorized her. On the one hand, she had the natural inclination to want to win this man's approval — to pass the test. On the other hand, she resented feeling that she was being sold as a slave in the market place. Yet to be completely honest, if this offer was turned down, she wanted to be the one doing the refusing. She was human. She didn't want to feel rejected.

When Saturday evening arrived, her apartment was immaculate. She had finally decided what to wear and was dressed with every hair in place. With 45 minutes yet to wait, every second was dragging. As the clock neared seven, she felt herself panic. "God, help me, please," came her whispered plea.

Finally the knock came at the door. Lucas had also been anticipating this moment with mixed excitement and dread. As he had watched his impossible dream evolve into a plausible possibility, he had begun to realize the lasting effects this change could have on his life. Sure, in his fantasy everything worked out perfectly, but by inserting the wrong woman he could be asking for a miserable existence for a while. She could take away any peace he might have in his home. She could drain his finances. She could irritate him to death. Yet one thing he would never let her do was get into his heart and break it … as Adrian had done.

Katie trembled slightly as she opened the door and looked up at Joe and the handsome stranger. The younger man was over six feet tall with dark hair and dark complexion. He was well built, with eyes that her mom might have called "dreamy". This split second appraisal threw Katie off balance. She had prepared herself to sympathize with a small, slightly balding widower who couldn't find a wife who would have him. Maybe she had thought that to prevent herself from being disappointed, but suddenly she wasn't sure how to act. This good looking, self assured man was exactly the kind of person who always intimidated her.

If she had known the truth, she would have realized that Lucas wasn't as self assured as he appeared. He, too, had been thrown by this first look at her. His expectations had envisioned finding a worldly wise woman who looked older than her years in a shabby, unkempt apartment. Instead, he was faced with an innocent looking young woman in a well-kept, though small, apartment that could best be described as homey. He felt a slight pang of guilt well up within, but he quickly quenched it. He would not let sympathy for this girl destroy his resolve. He wanted that job. He wanted his fantasy.

After Joe made the introduction and they were seated, Katie offered them coffee. Lucas didn't really want the coffee, but said "yes" because he wanted to see Katie in action. Since the tiny kitchen was open to the almost as tiny living room, Lucas could watch as she prepared the coffee and a snack. He could tell she was very nervous and suffered from his gaze, but she was comfortable in the kitchen. She knew what she was doing. With that fact and the cozy feel of her apartment, she passed the domesticity test.

Lucas utilized these moments to take a closer look at Katie's features. As he carefully judged her from head to toe, his initial reaction was confirmed. True, she was not glamorous like Adrian had been with her dark thick waves, her perfect figure, and the natural poise and sophistication many envied; but Katie was not hard on the eyes. She wasn't tall like Adrian. In fact, she was medium in every way: medium height, medium figure, medium brown hair, and medium brown eyes just as Joe had described her. The whole effect was quite nice. Her choice of clothes seemed perfect to Lucas ... casual, but not at all sloppy. The best part was that Lucas had the definite impression that she had not the slightest idea of how pretty she really was.

Once the coffee and homemade chocolate chip cookies were served, Lucas took the floor and began to ask questions. They were on paper, and he took written notes of her answers.

"Miss Montgomery, what is your full name?"

"Katlyn Marie Montgomery, but all my friends and family have always called me Katie."

"All right, Katlyn," Lucas continued, purposely using her formal name. "How old are you?"

"Twenty-three," her answer came quietly.

"And what about your family ... how many brothers and sisters do you have?"

"I have one brother, Mark, who is three years younger than I am."

"Where is he now?" Lucas continued to prod.

"He's at the University now, but he's joined the army and will be leaving in a few weeks."

Lucas's questions were confirming what Katie had suspected. Joe had told him nothing about her situation.

"Where do your parents live, Katlyn?" Lucas continued.

Katie's answer was brief but startling to Lucas. "My parents were killed in an automobile accident two years ago." Then, as if an afterthought, she continued, "I don't have any other close relatives."

Lucas felt that spark of guilt glimmer again, but once again he forced it down. He wasn't done with his interview.

"I'm sorry about your parents. That must have been very traumatic." Lucas replied, somewhat lamely.

"Let's see," he mumbled looking down at his notes. "Have you ever been married, Katlyn?"

"No!" the reply came with emphasis.

"How about engaged? Have you ever been engaged?"

"No," she answered simply.

"Do you have a boyfriend right now?"

"No," came the same answer.

At this point Lucas looked up with curiosity and asked a question apparently not on his list. "Why not, Katlyn? Why don't you have a boyfriend?"

This question flustered Katie. She'd in fact wondered the very same thing. Sure, over the years a few had seemed interested and she had dated a little, but she had never found anyone she was interested in getting serious about.

After an awkward pause she replied, "I guess because the right man has never come along."

This seemed to satisfy the interrogator, so he went on.

"Do you have any physical, mental, or emotional problems I should know about before entering into an agreement with you?"

"No," the answer came quickly. As Lucas watched Katie's eyes, he felt the quickness came from an honest belief that she had no hint of problem in those areas, not from an attempt to hide guilt.

As he took a moment now to consider all of Katie's answers and to look this young woman over again, he realized something that pleased him immensely. He was sure he could read this girl's eyes and if that were true, she could never hide anything from him.

Adrian had been so different. He could get lost in her eyes, yet never have the slightest idea what was really going on inside of her. That had been part of the mystique that had attracted Lucas to her, but after the marriage it had built a wall between them. In the end, that was what had been his ruination. Adrian had managed to carry on an affair without Lucas suspecting anything. But this girl was so easy to read; she'd have no secrets. How perfect!

It was obvious to Katie that Lucas was about done with this interview, but she hated the feeling that she was helpless and this stranger was totally in control. She wasn't going down without a fight.

"Excuse me," Katie forced herself to say. "I'd like to ask a few questions, also."

"Of course," Lucas replied confidently. But he really didn't like this turn. He wanted to stay in control.

Katie continued, trembling but determined. "What is your full name?"

"Lucas Michael Lehman."

"And how old are you, Mr. Lehman?"

"Twenty-nine," came the reply.

"Do you have any brothers or sisters or other family?"

Lucas went on without emotion. "No brothers or sisters. My parents divorced and remarried. Mother lives in New York, Dad in California."

Lucas could see the direction this interview had taken, but he could see no polite way out of it.

Katie forced herself to continue. "I understand you've been a widower for three years. Why have you never remarried?" Now she'd said it. She watched him carefully as he considered how to reply.

At first Lucas was taken aback. He had not thought she had the nerve to be so blunt. He certainly couldn't answer that question honestly to her or anyone else in the world. No one knew the bitterness he nurtured toward his dead wife and all women in general. Then a stroke of genius came to him. He replied with a very slight smile. "I guess because the right woman never came along."

Katie was not satisfied with this answer. She wondered if their marriage had been good or otherwise. Had he been so crushed by her death that he couldn't find anyone to replace her, or was he telling the truth. The right woman just hadn't crossed his path. She wasn't sure if it would make a difference to her final decision, but she wished she knew.

Mr. Lehman, "Do you have any physical, mental, or emotional problems I should be informed about?"

"No," the answer came quickly as Lucas' mind raced to the truth known only to him. There had been times during the last few years he had thought he was on the verge of insanity. This he would never reveal, and if all his plans worked out ... if his fantasy became a reality ... he was sure his problems would be over. What more could he ask for?

"I have one more question for you, Mr. Lehman," Katie continued. "Your proposition stated that if you are unsatisfied with the arrangement after a year, the marriage will be ended. What if you are satisfied, but I am not?"

Lucas considered the question as if that possibility had not crossed his mind. After some thought, he replied, "I guess the marriage would have to be dissolved."

Katie wanted to ask what would happen if he wanted to dissolve the marriage and she didn't, but she was sure she knew the answer to that, and she frankly didn't want to hear it spoken out loud.

With that last question, the interview seemed to be over. Both parties wished they knew more about what motivated the other, but this meeting would never reveal those answers. Only time would tell.

Joe, who had said nothing during the interview, began to speak. "Miss Montgomery, as you recall you need the money in just over a week, May 5th. Mr. Lehman is willing and able to make that payment for you, but only if the marriage takes place before that time. If you decide to agree to these arrangements, you must agree to marry him this next week."

At this point, Lucas spoke up, "My suggestion is that we fly to Reno next Friday." As he continued with his plan, he could read fear and shock in those expressive brown eyes.

"We could be married Friday evening. I'd make all the arrangements. We'd spend the night there, then come back Saturday in time for me to make your payment. I would leave you here for three or four weeks ... whatever time you would need to leave your work, dispose of your furniture, and do anything else you need to do before you leave town. Then you could fly to Chicago where I would pick you up at the airport."

It was only at this point that Lucas realized what he was saying. At some time during the interview, he had made his decision. He wanted a chance to make his "impossible dream" come true with this young woman.

As Lucas paused, Katie knew she should say something, but it was all happening too fast. She couldn't think. She felt as if she was going to suffocate.

"Joe, Mr. Lehman, I understand that I don't have much time, but I have to think this through alone. Is there some way I could give you my answer tomorrow?"

Lucas saw the panic in her eyes and struggled to ignore once again a feeling of guilt. Was it right to put this girl in this position? Wait a minute. She's the one that got herself in a bind by needing all that money. What could she have done to get herself in this position? No, he didn't really want to know. He didn't want the truth to lower his estimation of her, nor did he want to feel sympathy for her. Surely he was only helping her. She'd be well taken care of, live in a beautiful house and never have to work outside the home. What more could she ask for? He was sure that a lot of loveless marriages existed. She wouldn't have it so bad.

Joe looked at Lucas who answered, "I'll be here until tomorrow evening. My flight leaves at 9 P.M. Do you still have Joe's number? Just give him a call when you've made up your mind."

After the two men left, Katie curled up on the couch to ponder all the facts. She thought of the man she was considering the possibility of marrying. She had to admit that she had honestly never expected to marry a man as handsome as this stranger. She could imagine that he could be charming if he wanted to be, but his cold unemotional demeanor frightened her. Could she hope that it would change? Could she survive a life with him if it did not?

Yet did she have any choice right now? What alternatives did she have to protect her brother from some unknown hideous punishment or even death? Once again she tried to think of a way to get the money, but she'd already tried everything she knew. She honestly couldn't come up with any new ideas.

Katie picked up her telephone and dialed her brother's number.

"Mark, this is Katie," she began, but before she could say anything else, an agitated voice interrupted.

"Have those slime balls left yet?" he barked.

"Yes, they are gone."

"I should have come over there and knocked their blocks off … trying to take advantage of a bad situation like that."

"I think I'm going to go through with it, Mark," Katie plunged in.

"No way, Sis. That's crazy! We'll call the cops now. Surely there's something illegal about this proposition."

"Even if it were illegal, calling the police wouldn't keep them from getting to you. We just can't take that chance," Katie said firmly.

"No, Katie, there has to be another way! I won't let you do this," Mark objected.

"But we haven't come up with another way. I'm going to give them my answer tomorrow. Maybe it won't be that bad. Maybe it will all work out," she said unconvincingly. "I've made up my mind. It's the only thing I can do."

Now there was silence. After a few moments, Katie heard a sob at the other end and then in a broken voice the words, "I'm so sorry I've done this to you, Sis … so very sorry."

Then all she could hear was muffled sobbing and then suddenly the dial tone. Mark had hung up.

Now it was her turn to cry. She had been holding back the tears since the two men had left. Now all the tension and emotion of making this decision overwhelmed her as she released a river of tears. It felt as if her world was ending, and she had absolutely no hope for a respite. She normally cried very seldom, but she felt as if she deserved this one. So she sobbed until she was exhausted, then she fell asleep on the couch with a prayer on her lips. "Please, God, help me."

CHAPTER 6

At the brief meeting the next day, Katie and Lucas both signed their names at the bottom of two copies of the agreement. Katie doubted there was anything really legal about signing this document, but she did take it seriously. She would do her best to abide by the requirements. Lucas handed her a signed copy then purposefully placed five one hundred dollar bills in her hand. When she looked confused, he just said, "This is to buy something nice to wear for next Friday… nothing fancy … just something appropriate. If you have anything left over, use it for whatever else you need. I'll call next week to let you know exactly when I'll pick you up." With that said, he was out the door and gone.

The next days passed like a dream. Her employer was shocked when she gave her two weeks notice, but the girls she worked with were ecstatic when she shyly informed him that she was getting married. She was thankful that an unusually-heavy workload that week made extra chit chat impossible. She rushed out after work, explaining that she had so much to do, she couldn't stay and talk.

She hoped everyone was convinced that she was excitedly looking forward to wedded bliss. Yet, somehow, Patti sensed something was amiss. Patti was different from the rest. She was thoughtful and kind to everyone even when they didn't deserve it. Katie figured it was because of Patti's religion. She had tried to explain her beliefs to Katie more than once, but Katie had never paid much attention. She just couldn't see the need to worry about it. She wasn't a bad person, and hadn't she gotten through the crisis with her parents' death all right? Surely that was God helping her, so she must be okay.

Right now, Patti's kind consideration both drew Katie and made her slightly uncomfortable. She had certainly recognized a need for God's help recently, but if she asked Patti for advice, she'd have to tell her something about what was going on in her life, and she couldn't bring herself to do that. So she kept her distance from everyone including Patti. Last week, Patti had invited her to some sort of week long meetings at her church, starting next Sunday. Maybe she would try to make it one night. Patti had invited her so many times during the last three years, and she'd never made it. She took the flier home that listed the times and the address. She'd just have to see what she felt like next week.

Friday came too quickly. She took the day off to make some final purchases, get her hair done, and get ready for Lucas' arrival at 5 P.M. The dress she found for the occasion was soft and silky in a pale pastel. She wasn't sure it would pass Lucas' definition of appropriate, but the new outfit made her feel very feminine.

Mark came by around four in the afternoon to wish her well, but she insisted he leave before Lucas arrived. She could envision Mark shaking hands with Lucas and then punching him. She was nervous enough and shooed him away by 4:30. Just as she was closing the suitcase for the overnight trip, she heard a knock at the door.

Once again her heart leaped, and she felt the fear that had become her companion so often during the past few weeks. She took a slow deep breath, then opened the door for Lucas.

He looked very striking in a dark sports coat and bright blue shirt with matching tie. Yet she felt that his good looks only accentuated her plainness. Surely the justice of the peace would think this man could do better. She sighed in resignation. She had done the best she knew how with her looks. Was he disappointed?

Lucas had been bursting with anticipation all week. It was hard to believe that something born in his imagination during those lonely, restless evenings was actually coming true. As he saw her standing just inside the door looking all soft and silky, his anticipation soared to even greater heights. All this was hidden behind an unemotional facade. As he took a long look at this young woman who was soon to become his wife, he was surprised by the sudden urge to reach up and touch the loose curl by her cheek. Outwardly he was all business now, asking her if she was ready for the trip.

Katie smile weakly, "Yes, I'll just check to make sure the lights are all out."

She stepped into her bedroom, thinking that her life would never be the same. When she returned, she would be married. Her world would be different forever. What mammoth changes were awaiting her just around the corner? There was no time to ponder it all now. Lucas was waiting. She was trying very hard to think of this husband-to-be as Lucas. She had never called him that. Mr. Lehman had always felt more appropriate. She so wished she could feel more at ease with him, but there was such a wall of ice between them. Would it ever melt?

Both the trip to the airport and the flight itself were uncomfortably quiet for Katie. In a way the silence was a blessing because she had not the slightest idea what to say to this man. She felt so very much alone gazing down at the fluffy white clouds below her. She could almost imagine that she was the only person in the whole world. The loneliness almost hurt.

As she closed her eyes, a picture came into her mind of what she had always imagined this day would be like ... a flowing white dress, delicate veil, bouquet of roses, handsome groom with eyes full of love. She realized only now that she would never experience any of this. When she felt a teardrop overflow and drop onto her cheek, she quickly turned away so Lucas couldn't see.

Lucas had seen and was struggling to maintain his stoic mindset on this marriage arrangement. He had been so elated at the way his fantasy was falling into place that he had not even considered Katie's feelings about the quick and unromantic wedding. Well, it was better for her to understand the way things were from the start. Besides, all that sentimental stuff was a bunch of malarkey anyway. He'd had all that with his first wedding and what did it get him? Unbelievable misery had been his reward. No, he refused to be sorry for not playing the game of romance. It was better not to get her hopes up because this was going to be a marriage of convenience with none of the emotional baggage a normal relationship brings.

By this time, another thought had struck Katie. Here she was on her way to marry this stranger, but how did she know he would go back and pay Joe the money Mark owed. He could forcibly take her to his home and never pay a penny. Mark could still end up maimed for life or even dead. Why had she been stupid enough to agree to this order of events? She should have demanded payment first, and then she could have faced her fate knowing her brother would be all right. What could she do now? How could she be sure about anything? The only facts she knew about this man were his name and age ... if Lucas Michael Lehman was his real name. For all she knew, he could be a thief or a gangster or a murderer. Maybe he even murdered his first wife.

"Wait a minute, Katlyn Marie Montgomery," she thought to herself. "Let's not get carried away. Pull yourself together."

Katie calmed herself but was still concerned for her brother's welfare. She took a deep breath, mustered up all the courage she could, then broke the silence.

"Lucas," she said quietly as if trying out the name, "When will you see Joe to make the payment?"

"So that's all she's worried about?" was the first thought that leaped into Lucas' mind. "I should have guessed," he mused.

"Don't worry, Babe," he answered with a touch of bitterness, "You'll get your money. Joe is meeting us at around six tomorrow evening at your apartment to collect the tidy sum. You just make sure you're worth it."

With that Lucas lapsed back into silence, reprimanding himself for expecting more from a bride he had to pay $35,000 to get.

Katie felt the full intensity of the bitter reply. She quickly turned her head to the window to hide tears of hurt and shame at being trapped in this nightmare. Closing her eyes, she tried to sleep to escape the frightening thoughts that were tormenting her.

As she fell into a troubled sleep, her head found a resting place on Lucas' shoulder. He unconsciously adjusted his position to make her more comfortable. She looked so innocent, yet he reminded himself that all she was concerned about was the money. What kind of woman would need $35,000 so much she would agree to marry a total stranger? He had to be on his guard, or he would start feeling sorry for her. In spite of all his attempts at caution, it felt good to feel her pretty little head rest against him.

When the flight attendant began preparing for the landing, Lucas gently nudged Katie. She opened her eyes to find Lucas staring at her. He noticed that lost kitten look again and gave up his resolve to be angry at her preoccupation with money.

With little conversation, Katie found herself whisked from the airport to a luxurious suite in a large hotel. She was tempted to fear that Lucas intended to skip the wedding ceremony, but he caught the look in her eye and quickly spoke up to reassure her.

"You go ahead in and freshen up. We have about thirty minutes before we have to leave to make it to the chapel in time for our appointment."

Lucas decided that there was more than one way to freshen up. He made his way down to the bar for a drink or two. He needed something to drown the memories which kept trying to surface … memories of another wedding day … another woman … memories that always ended in bitterness, regret, and hatred.

CHAPTER 7

The chapel was quaint, but the ceremony was definitely a commercial affair. The small bouquet of delicate roses that Lucas purchased for his shy bride appeared to curious onlookers to be an offer of love. "What a sweet couple!" was the passing thought of the bystanders. Katie knew his true motives … to legitimize the appearance of the loveless union. Why he cared what these strangers thought, she didn't comprehend. Now at least she didn't have to wonder what to do with her hands.

When it was time to repeat the vows, Katie surprised Lucas by looking directly into his eyes and saying each phrase with deliberate meaning. In spite of the circumstances, she desperately wanted a marriage that would blossom and last a lifetime. She tried to grasp at a fleeting hope that this could be a real marriage.

It was Katie's turn to be surprised when Lucas slipped on an exquisitely engraved wedding band with delicate flowers surrounding a medium sized sparkling diamond. He handed her a plain gold band to put on his finger.

When the justice of the peace said, "You may kiss the bride," Lucas gently pulled her close and gave her a lingering kiss that surprised them both. No one there could have suspected that they were two strangers brought together by outlandish circumstances. In those moments they looked like a young couple deeply in love, but the spell was soon broken. They walked out the door, her arm in his then at once felt mutually uncomfortable with the closeness.

After signatures and formalities, Lucas suggested they go for dinner. Katie agreed meekly, feeling sure she couldn't eat a bite, but willing to do anything to postpone their trip back to the hotel room.

The dinner was quiet and awkward. Lucas ate his favorite meal without even tasting it. Katie spent most of the time fingering the beautiful ring on her hand.

"I'm sorry the ring is too large," Lucas apologized. "You'll have to have it made smaller next week." Lucas had assumed Katie would wear the same size as Adrian. He had been shocked when he put the ring on her tiny finger.

"That's all right," she offered. "My hands are small. There is no way you could have known. I want to thank you for the ring, though. I've never seen such a beautiful and unique wedding band. How did you find such a lovely ring?"

Lucas was warmed by her honest appreciation of his choice. Adrian had never liked his taste. He had given up trying to surprise her with jewelry or perfumes. She inevitably returned his gifts for something she liked better.

This was a new experience. He had walked into a leading jewelers last week, determined not to worry about which ring to buy. When his eyes fell on this delicately carved band, Katie's face had momentarily flashed through his mind. He had congratulated himself that he just took the first ring he saw, refusing to admit to himself that there was more to it than that. Now he felt rewarded by seeing her look of gratitude when she spoke of the ring. All at once he was anxious to return to the hotel. He had successfully squelched any guilt about this marriage and was looking forward to this first night with his pretty new bride.

Katie, on the other hand, grew more uneasy the closer they got to their suite. When they entered the room, she fought the fear that was welling up deep in the pit of her stomach. Lucas sensed her fear and saw her confusion, but he wasn't afraid or confused.

He closed the door, locked it, then took purposeful steps to Katie's side. In only a moment, she found herself in his arms being aggressively kissed and caressed as she had never been before. Yet even as she kissed him back, she couldn't help thinking how odd this seemed. Only a few moments ago they were strangers. She had to remind herself that they were married, and there was nothing wrong with what they were doing. Maybe things would work out after all.

Later that night, long after Katie had gone to sleep beside him, Lucas once again struggled with his thoughts. He couldn't deny that he had enjoyed the evening immensely. It had been three years since he had been close to a woman, and except for the brief moments when Adrian had flashed through his mind, the experience had been satisfying. Yet now after it was over, he was confused again. He had discovered something he had not expected. Katie had been a virgin. This possibility had not even crossed his mind. Not even Adrian had been a virgin. Lucas had assumed that the kind of woman who would agree to marry for a sum of money must be worldly … not an innocent girl. Who was this woman? Why was she with him in this hotel tonight? What forced her into this? No, he didn't really want to know. He planned on enjoying this platonic marriage and getting out of it all he could, so he didn't want anything to make him feel guilty. No emotional baggage … that was the plan, and he intended to follow it, no matter what.

When Katie awoke the next morning, she hoped to find a warm, loving mate, but to her amazement the wall between them was back up. Lucas was polite but formal, much as he had been before the ceremony. Katie hid her disappointment as she dressed and prepared to leave the hotel.

Once again the flight was quiet, but at least she was getting used to it. Not until they were back in Katie's apartment did Lucas strike up an actual conversation. All the way back he had been considering the next few weeks. Originally he had planned to give Katie a month to get her affairs in order, but now he was having second thoughts. He liked having her around and didn't really want to wait a month to take her to his home.

"How long will it take you to get everything done so you can move up to my place?" Lucas started in abruptly.

Katie, startled by the sudden question after so long a silence stuttered, "Well, uh ... well, I ... I don't know exactly. It depends on what I find to do with my furniture, and I still have one more week at work and, well, I don't really know."

Lucas thought for a moment before continuing, "I guess I'll give you a call later this week. Maybe you'll have a better idea by then. I'd like to get things taken care of and have you settled at my house as soon as you can finalize arrangements here."

"All right," Katie started, but just then Joe was knocking at the door.

"And how are the newlyweds," Joe boomed, giving Lucas a sly smile and Katie a wink. "Did everything go smoothly?"

"Without a hitch," Lucas responded with a reserved smile.

"Well, if you're satisfied, we'd better take care of the little lady's payment. My employer is not a very patient man."

Again Joe winked at Katie with a chuckle that brought a blush to her cheeks. Lucas seemed to enjoy Katie's discomfort as he opened a worn attaché case and produced two certified checks.

"Will this meet with your employer's approval?" Lucas responded.

Katie was confused with two checks instead of one. She had no idea that Joe had included $10,000 for himself in this transaction. Lucas assumed the entire $35,000 was Katie's debt but was to cover two separate payments requiring two checks. Joe inspected each check and then stashed them in his suit coat pocket. His business transacted, Joe wished them luck in their newly found marital bliss and made a quick exit before Katie had the chance to ask any questions about the two checks. But before he'd reached his car, he saw Katie running to catch him. He squirmed inwardly as he put on a big smile and turned to face her.

"Joe, now you promise me this is all over. No one will harm my brother ever again. Promise me, Joe."

There was such a sweet sincerity in her voice, Joe hastened to reassure her. "Now don't you worry your poor little head, Missy. Your brother doesn't have a worry in the world ... as long as he gives up gambling permanently. Maybe Uncle Sam will straighten him up in the army."

Katie was only partly reassured when she realized that Joe knew that Mark had enlisted. "I guess I should thank you for working out something for me." Katie stated slowly.

Joe interrupted boisterously, anxious to leave before the subject of checks came up. "Well, you sure are the lucky girl, getting a fine good looking man like Lucas Lehman. That boy has a big house and lots of money, too. I'm glad I could be of service. I've got to run now, Missy. You know my employer doesn't like to be kept waiting."

And with that, he was in his car and driving away. As Katie slowly walked back across the parking lot to her building, she pondered what Joe had said about a big house, money, and a handsome husband. Would she ever be really happy again?

Lucas left soon after Katie came back into her apartment. "This is for any expenses you might incur while preparing to move up to Chicago," he said as he placed ten 100 dollar bills and a credit card in her hand. "I also want you to buy a new wardrobe, new hairstyle, whatever you want. As my wife you'll be representing me, so I want you to look like Mrs. Lucas Lehman. Use the money where they won't take a card."

"No, Lucas," Katie finally broke in. "This isn't necessary. I'll have another paycheck or two coming. I can take care of anything I need."

"Don't worry, Katlyn. I've got plenty," he smiled. "I'm sure you can find something to do with it."

"But I ..." was all she got out before Lucas opened the door.

"Goodbye for now. I'll call next Friday," and then he was gone. Katie was dumbfounded. She hid the money in her dresser drawer and put the credit card in her billfold. What was this man really like? Was he being kind, or was he just concerned that she would embarrass him with her own clothes? Oh, well, why worry about it? She might as well just enjoy this unexpected pleasure. She'd have to start her shopping right after work on Monday.

CHAPTER 8

As Katie walked into her small kitchen her eyes fell on the flyer Patti had given her.

OLD FASHIONED REVIVAL
AND EVANGELISTIC MEETINGS
May 7-12
Come Hear Norm Donaldson
Preach the Word

It all sounded kind of quaint, but maybe that's just what she needed to get her mind off what was going on in her life right now. Wouldn't Patti be surprised? There was a service at 11:00 A.M. Sunday morning. She'd give it a try. It wasn't even that far from her apartment.

As she fixed a simple supper and sat down to eat, she thought about her coworker Patti. How could you describe Patti? For one thing … different … but not in a bad way. She had just never known anyone else like her. Katie supposed Patti was reasonably pretty, but when you thought of Patti it wasn't what was on the outside that came to mind. She had sort of an inner beauty. True, some of the other girls snickered at her and called her a "fanatic" behind her back, but Katie never quite understood what they meant. Personally she had wished she could be more like Patti. She never got preachy or looked down her nose at anyone, but everyone knew there were certain things Patti would not do under any circumstances like lie or be dishonest in any way. She never gossiped about the others, even though she knew they did about her. Oh, she was no angel. She'd gotten upset before over unfair treatment in the office, but she was always quick to apologize when she thought she might have offended a coworker. Many times Katie observed Patti just forgive and forget when someone had been unkind to her.

Katie asked her once how she could take it so well when others mistreated her. She said she had a friend with whom she shared her problems, and he had promised to work everything out for her good in the end. When Katie laughed and asked to be introduced to this wonder working friend, Patti had said her friend's name was Jesus, and she'd love to introduce her to Him. Katie was slightly embarrassed and found a reason to leave immediately, but she still inwardly marveled at the familiar way Patti talked about Jesus.

Anyway, she was sure Patti would be thrilled to see her walk into her church, and it would be nice to make her friend happy before Katie moved out of town.

The church Katie entered the next morning was not very big. The board at the back of the church said there were 97 people in Sunday School last week, but she was sure there were a lot more here now. Others besides Patti must have invited their friends because of the special speaker.

She was disappointed that she didn't see Patti anywhere, so she sat in a pew close to the back of the church. She felt uncomfortable all by herself and was thinking maybe she shouldn't have come. It had been a long time since she had been to church, and the last one she visited had been very solemn and formal. As she looked around at this little congregation, many were smiling, chatting with each other and even laughing out loud. It didn't seem very dignified, but they certainly looked happy. Many of these strangers had already welcomed her and introduced themselves.

When the service finally started, Katie realized why she hadn't found Patti. She looked up to see her co-worker standing in the choir. Patti had seen her and was beaming. Just as Katie had suspected, her friend looked overjoyed to see her there.

The service proceeded with songs, announcements, an offering and prayers. The prayers caught her attention. They weren't memorized or read. Neither were they flowery or poetic, but they were sincere ... just as if the men who were praying were really talking to someone.

After one more song, Katie was surprised to watch Patti leave the choir loft and stand in front of the church with a microphone. How perfect! She was going to sing a solo. Katie listened carefully to the words as Patti sang in a clear, sweet voice.

Katie missed most of the second verse. She was too busy pondering the words to the first. It sounded as if the song was talking about her life with so much private pain and hidden fears. Did Patti suspect something was going on? Did she sing that just for her? Of course not! She didn't even know Katie was coming, but the similarity of this song to her present situation seemed uncanny.

After Patti's solo, the choir was seated in the audience, and Patti came back to sit by her. Following an exchange of whispered greeting, they settled back to listen. Katie was delighted to find the speaker quite interesting. He kept incorporating experiences from his past into his talk to make the story come alive. She didn't know the Bible could be this relevant.

He kept talking about a man named Cornelius. She had never heard of him before. He apparently was religious; he had a reverence for God; he gave to charity; he was honest, had a good reputation, and prayed regularly. Well, she could certainly see why the preacher was using him as an example. He surely put her to shame. But the speaker was saying one more thing about this wonderful man. Wait a minute! Did she hear that right? Did he say Cornelius was going to Hell? How could that be? But the preacher was saying that some guy named Peter was sent by God to tell this man and his family how to be saved. How unbelievable! Yet she read the words right in Patti's Bible. That's really what it said. Where did that leave her if a man like that wasn't even going to heaven? The preacher said Cornelius needed to hear the Gospel. Now what does that mean?

Yet this Norm Donaldson fellow wasn't talking about that. He was talking about what the Gospel was not. Katie wished she could write some of this down. She'd never remember it all. Then she noticed Patti was taking notes. Good! Maybe she could borrow her notes to copy for herself. She'd just relax and listen. The first thing he said was the Gospel was not "love your neighbor as yourself." Nor was it turning over a new leaf or reforming yourself. It wasn't obeying the ten commandments or doing good works or church membership. His list kept growing. but Katie had lapsed into sort of a daze, trying to fathom what she had already heard. He'd already listed everything she could imagine that would be labeled as the True Gospel.

Katie wished he'd get to the punch line. What was the "Gospel" that could "save" a person anyway? Then he was talking about Jesus coming from heaven to earth for us. He talked about how His death, burial, and resurrection was the good news we needed to hear … that once Cornelius heard about this and believed Jesus had done all that to pay for his sins, he accepted the gift of salvation and was saved.

This was all so new to Katie. She'd heard about Jesus all her life and how He died on the cross and rose again, and she'd always assumed it was true. It was a historical fact after all. Yet she was sure it was more that a historical fact to Patti and those sitting around her.

The preacher then invited any who wanted to receive Christ today to walk up front where he was standing and let someone show him or her how. Katie had a strange uncomfortable feeling that she should do that, but she resisted. Not now. She'd have to think more about this. She held on to the pew ahead of her and stood firm. She looked at Patti standing beside her. She had her eyes closed. Surely Patti didn't have the same odd feeling she did.

After the service, Patti introduced Katie to several girls about their age, two of which were her roommates. They were all going out to eat together and insisted Katie join them. She felt as if she might be intruding, but she didn't want to go back to her apartment alone, so she agreed.

For a while, Katie envied their carefree spirit and thought that they probably didn't have a care in the world, but as the meal progressed, in spite of the laughing and teasing, she realized from the conversation that they each had their own problems, also. One girl named Hannah was concerned for her mother who was apparently dying of cancer. Sandy, who had beautiful auburn hair, was missing her fiancé who was overseas in the Air Force. How was it that they all seemed to have such peace? Could it be that Jesus was their friend as Patti had said, and He promised each of them that He would work things out for her good? Katie surely wished she had some hope like that, but she didn't. Behind her own smile she felt totally hopeless … empty … kind of like that song Patti had sung.

After lunch, Katie left her new acquaintances and started for home, but not until they had extracted a promise from her that she would return to their church for the evening service at seven.

All afternoon Katie pondered what she had heard and seen that day. This was the first time in her entire life she had considered the possibility that doing her best wasn't enough to please God or to get her to heaven. Her parents had worked hard to instill in her some character, a standard of right and wrong, morality. She had remained a virgin when many of her high school friends had not. Yet if what she heard about that fellow Cornelius was true, that just doing her best wasn't enough, then she was in trouble. She had grown up assuming the Bible was true. Her parents had rarely opened a Bible, but she never doubted that whatever was in there was to be believed.

Katie pondered Patti and her friends. As she contemplated all this, cuddled up on her couch, she dozed off. The next thing she knew she was engulfed in a thick fog, trying to find her way to a voice she could hear calling her name. Fear mounted as she searched for someone to help her. Then she recognized that the voice was Patti. Finally the haze began to disperse, and she strained to locate the source of the sound.

Katie woke with a start. Patti's voice was on the other side of the door.

"Are you in there, Katie? Is anything wrong?" Patti sounded concerned.

Jumping up suddenly, Katie let her friend into the apartment. "I'm sorry, Patti, I must have fallen asleep. I didn't hear you knock. Oh dear, what time is it? I'm not ready yet."

"No problem," Patti reassured her. "I'm early. Can you be ready in ten or fifteen minutes?"

"Sure, have a seat. I'll be ready in a flash."

Patti had agreed to stop by and pick Katie up. The idea appealed to Katie because then she wouldn't have to walk in alone. As far as Patti was concerned, this was her best guarantee that her friend would come back.

True to her word, Katie was ready in no time, and they were in the church and seated well before the meeting started. The service was different that night ... more relaxed. The crowd was smaller but friendly. Many remembered

Katie from the morning and welcomed her back. Katie was warmed by their sincerity.

Even the tone of the sermon was much different. The speaker was talking about David and Goliath tonight. At least Katie was familiar with them. He talked about how David had learned to trust the Lord over the years because he had experienced God's power while watching his father's sheep. Katie never realized David had already killed a lion and a bear before he ever faced the giant Goliath. As the audience sat listening to the account which was interspersed with private illustrations, they laughed and then fought back tears. The emphasis was for God's children to serve Him courageously because David's God was their God, also.

Though Katie laughed and cried with the rest, she realized from the start that this sermon was not for her. It was for these people who somehow knew God personally. She couldn't expect God's help because He was a stranger. As she sat and listened, she sincerely wanted to know God. She needed Him, and she wanted His friendship.

This time when the preacher invited those who weren't sure of where they would spend eternity to come down to the front, Katie paused only for a moment, then shyly moved out and down the aisle. A smiling, soft spoken woman in her early forties took Katie into a side room and explained to her again her need to make a decision. She showed her from the Bible that she was a sinner and that Jesus was her only hope of receiving God's forgiveness. After a brief conversation, Katie bowed her head and meekly asked Jesus to forgive her for her sins, thanking Him for paying the penalty for her when He died on the cross. She asked Him quietly to come into her life and be her Savior. Before she closed, with tears she thanked Jesus for saving her. When she opened her eyes, she saw the other woman's eye were glistening.

She responded to Patti's beaming face with a quiet, "I did it. Now Jesus is my friend, too."

"I'm so happy for you, Katie. This is a real answer to prayer," Patti said with emotion.

Katie was incredulous. "You prayed for me?"

"I've been praying for you for at least two years, but especially the last few weeks. God just kept bringing you to my mind and impressing me to pray for you." With those words she gave Katie a warm hug.

How long had it been since Katie had felt the touch of a caring friend? She hugged Patti back and marveled at how good she felt. For so long it had seemed that no one other than her brother Mark cared much whether she lived or died. She hadn't been that depressed about it. It just seemed to be a fact of her life. How comforting it was to realize that Patti had cared and even God had cared. She had a peace that she had never known before.

CHAPTER 9

The change Katie felt the next day as she entered the office was incredible. For one thing she was married now, though she didn't really feel like it. No one else knew she was already married, not even Patti. She just couldn't bring herself to tell people yet. It would be too hard to explain how it all came about so soon. They weren't aware of Mark's gambling and all the problems it brought, and she didn't want them to know. She desperately hoped that none of them would ever comprehend that she was forced into this marriage.

Even more important than her new marital status was her newfound relationship with Jesus Christ. She truly did feel different inside, but she was unsure about how to act around her coworkers. She wanted to say something but couldn't think of how to start.

During her lunch hour, she took her wedding band to a jeweler to have it made smaller. It was a relief to have a legitimate reason not to wear it even though it was truly lovely. Then over a quick lunch, she pondered what she would do after work to begin getting ready to make the move. There was so much to be done. She had to make arrangements to break her lease. Next was the task of packing up all her belongings. Finally she had to find something to do with most of her possessions, including her furniture. She was sure she should not bring much of her old things to Lucas' home. She couldn't bear the thought of disposing of many of her keepsakes, but what was she going to do with all of it?

Of course, she had to shop for new things as Lucas had requested. That should be fun except she was concerned that maybe her new husband wouldn't like her choices. Where should she begin?

Katie returned to work, still unsure of what she'd do this evening. Then Patti asked her if she'd be back to the special meetings that night, and her mind was made up. That was one thing she really wanted to do. She'd pack what she could for a couple of hours then go to the church.

The rest of the week went by like a blur. The days at work flew because there were so many loose ends she wanted to tie up before she left the job. The girls at the office even had a bridal shower for her Friday afternoon. Each evening she did some shopping or packing before and after going to the special meetings at the church. There were sermons on prayer, the home, and prophecy. Katie even talked her brother into coming with her on Friday night. She knew that he was starting a new life in the military and needed Jesus as much as she did. But Mark obviously didn't understand what it was all about. It was all too new to him.

The young adults of the church had a relaxing time of games and snacks after the service on Friday night. It was at this time Katie learned they had just finished remodeling an area in the church basement to accommodate speakers like Evangelist Norm Donaldson as well as missionaries traveling through their area. When Katie went with the others to see the fine construction work, she noticed they had no furniture. She inquired and discovered that they were looking for good used furniture to put into service for the Lord. Katie couldn't believe her ears. She had an apartment full of furniture that needed a home. Before the evening was over, she had explained that she was moving soon and donated all her furniture. Patti had offered to store Katie's keepsakes in her attic indefinitely. Her car, which wasn't really worth much, would be donated to a mission for the homeless.

Katie returned to her apartment, feeling comforted that Jesus already seemed to be working things out for her good. Patti had shown her where that verse was in the second hand Bible she had given her. Katie chuckled as she thought about Patti's explanation when she handed her the beautiful burgundy Bible. "My parents gave me a new Bible for my birthday, and my old one wasn't worn out at all."

What had struck Katie funny was the thought that anyone would read a Bible enough to wear it out. The only Bible Katie had owned was a huge family Bible with all the family births, deaths, and marriages written in it. Even though she was the fourth generation in the family to own it, there was very little wear showing. They had always kept it in a box and rarely brought it out except to write a date in it. The only time Katie actually remembered reading from it was when she was about ten years old. Aunt Rhonda had come to their home for Christmas and insisted they read the story of the nativity before they opened their gifts. Mark had been irritable and eager to open his presents, but Katie had sat dreamily, liking the sound of the reading even though a lot of the language seemed almost foreign.

Now as Katie leafed through the pages trying to find Romans 8:28, she determined she would wear this Bible out. Patti had many verses underlined and notes written in the margins. Finally she found the verse she was looking for and read it aloud. "And we know that God causes all things to work together for good to those who love God ..."

As she read that last word, the telephone startled her. She picked up the phone to hear an irritated voice. "Where have you been? Why were you out so late?"

It was Lucas. She had forgotten he was to call tonight. Conflicting feelings bombarded her. So much had happened since their wedding one week ago. She felt so different, yet one thing had not changed. She was still Lucas' wife, but she couldn't understand why he was so upset. It was only about 10:30 at night.

Lucas had started calling about seven that evening and had been calling every half an hour since then. All sorts of things had gone through his mind when she didn't answer again and again, but the one thought that kept reoccurring was that Katie had left town. He had paid $35,000 for nothing. He would never see or hear from her again. Lucas kept telling himself that this woman didn't mean anything to him; he just hated to be taken. But the truth was that he had enjoyed last weekend and was anxiously waiting to see her again. He still wanted his fantasy and Katie was the fulfillment of it.

After a slight pause, Katie answered, quietly, "I was out with some friends."

"Didn't you remember I was to call tonight?" Lucas spit back.

Another pause came, then a quieter, "No, I guess I didn't."

"Well you're going to have to remember what I say to you in the future. You're not getting off to a very good start in our arrangement." Lucas really didn't want to be this short-tempered, but he had gotten so worked up the last few hours that he couldn't stop himself from thoughtlessly venting his frustration. This really wasn't how he wanted this conversation to go. He took a deep breath and changed the subject.

"How are things going? How soon will you be ready to move?" Lucas attempted to change his tone.

Katie was hurt. Moving in with this man was the last thing she wanted to think about at this moment.

"Well, uh, I'm not sure," Katie stammered. "I've found a place for my furniture, and I've started packing things away and I've done a little shopping, but there's still much that has to be done."

Again Lucas' voice sounded annoyed. "You're not planning to bring a bunch of worthless, sentimental junk to clutter up my house, are you?"

Once again Katie felt the sting. Once again she paused before she quietly answered, "No, of course not."

There was silence on both ends. Lucas knew this whole conversation had been a giant blunder on his part, but Katie had remained meek. He soothed his conscience by thinking this was a good test of her character. From this "test" he could envision her fitting into his fantasy. So surely he hadn't really done anything wrong.

Katie didn't speak because she couldn't. She was close to tears and was fighting to maintain control.

Lucas had another thought. "You're finished up at your job now, aren't you?"

"Yes," was all Katie could manage.

"Good," Lucas said with emphasis. "You'll have more time to get things ready. I'll call in a few days and see how things are progressing. Goodbye."

"Goodbye."

When she put the phone down, she just let herself cry. That short telephone conversation had somehow crushed her spirit. She had been so happy for six days. How could a few minutes destroy her peace?

As she lifted her head, she saw her opened Bible on the couch beside her. Picking it up, she repeated the words she had read just before the call.

"And we know that in all things God works for the good of those who love him ..."

She really did love God. What was it the pastor's wife had told her one night last week ... something about all the promises in the Bible? Oh, yes, it was that if these promises seemed impossible, she would just have to make a choice to believe God whether she felt like it or not. She was not to trust her feelings but to trust Jesus and what He said in His Word.

"All right, Lord," she said out loud. "Here is the first impossible promise I've faced. I don't see any way You can take this terrible mess I'm in and work it out for good, but I do love You, so I guess You have to work it out. I choose to believe You ... and while You're at it, could You please help me be strong when I go to live with Lucas? I don't want to spend the rest of my life in tears. Thanks, Lord, I feel better already."

And she did. Somehow she and the Lord would make it. Just then she remembered something she had picked up at the store during her lunch break. After picking up her wedding band (which was still in her purse), she had stopped at the Card and Gift Shop next door to the jewelers and picked up a journal. When the evangelist had spoken on prayer, he had mentioned that it was a good idea to make a prayer list and also to write down answers to your prayers. She found the shopping bag, pulled out the journal, and began to write. Somehow it seemed to come out more like a letter to the Lord than a prayer list. It was kind of like a diary, but instead of "Dear Diary" it was "Dear Lord."

By the time she crawled into bed, her peace had returned.

"Good night, Lord," she said sleepily. "Thanks for everything."

Even though Katie wasn't working anymore, the days still flew by. She divided her time between lovingly packing her sentimental keepsakes, packing up many things to give away to charity, and shopping for a new wardrobe. She even got her hair cut in a new style.

Though it had been time consuming to go through everything she owned to decide what to do with it, she marveled at how smoothly everything was going. Surely God was helping her as she had been requesting daily, but this brought another problem. The sooner she got things settled, the sooner she would have to move away from the town where she had spent her entire life. She trembled every time she pondered the idea. At the rate things were going, she'd be ready to move by the end of the week.

Wednesday evening Katie came home from prayer meeting just in time to hear the phone ring. She breathed a call for help heavenward as she picked up the receiver.

"Hello," she said quietly.

"You've been out again," the slightly-irritated voice said.

"Yes, I have," was all Katie replied.

"Well, where were you so late on a Wednesday night."

"It's only eight forty-five."

"Oh, so you don't want to tell me where you were?"

Katie answered slowly, "I was at church."

Lucas was silent. Nothing like this had ever crossed his mind. He wondered if she could be some kind of religious fanatic. He hoped not. That could ruin his fantasy. He wasn't sure why, but it just didn't seem to fit.

He changed the subject. "How's your packing and shopping going? Are you ready to fly out here?"

"Not quite," she tried to sound a little cheery. "I have a few more things to do. How does Sunday night sound?" She closed her eyes and held her breath, waiting for the answer. She could be ready sooner, but she wanted one more Sunday here with her new friends at church.

Lucas' answer was not enthusiastic. "If that's the best you can do...By the way, box up most of your things and send them on ahead. Then you won't have to deal with them on the airplane. My address is 10304 N. Sycamore Drive, Bedford, Illinois.

"Okay, Lucas, I'll do that. If you give me your telephone number, I'll call and tell you what flight I'm coming in on."

"The number is 329/555-4789. Let me know tomorrow. Goodbye, Katlyn."

Well, there it was. She had four days left.

CHAPTER 10

On Friday Katie spent the evening with her brother, Mark. Sitting across from each other at an Italian restaurant, they reminisced about old times as they were growing up together. They laughed a lot and cried a little, missing their parents much and contemplating the life they were both leaving far behind. They sat silently for a few moments, pondering the changes they were both facing in the immediate future.

Mark spoke first. "You know, Sis, you've changed a lot the last few weeks. It's terrible to think, but it seems as if all this pressure and the nightmare I brought on you changed you for the better. Dad always said that problems build character. I guess it must be true because you seem to have more courage and peace the last couple of weeks than you ever had before."

Katie paused as she considered her answer. "I guess, in a way, all this mess had something to do with whatever change you are seeing, but it's not exactly the way you think. All my life up until Mom and Dad died, I was pretty comfortable. I knew I wasn't perfect, but compared to a lot of people, I figured I rated pretty well. Now that I look back, I realize that I have our parents to thank for what I was. They loved me, taught me, and disciplined me so I learned to make some right choices. When Mom and Dad died, I cried out to God for help, but when I got through it all, I kind of figured I had been strong enough to overcome adversity by myself. I didn't give God any credit for helping. Yet that crisis was different than this one. I just had to keep on going, one day at a time, doing what I knew had to be done.

"But when things started going wrong a few weeks ago … your beating, finding out about the gambling, not being able to come up with the money … I didn't have any answers. I had no one to go to and no idea what to do. Then when Lucas came along with his offer, and I suddenly found myself married to a complete stranger … well, you can imagine how helpless I felt.

"It was then I decided to visit Patti's church. I heard about this remarkable guy named Cornelius. He did all sorts of really good deeds. He put me to shame; that's for sure, but when I found out he still needed to be saved, I was floored. I thought, 'If he isn't good enough to please God, who is?' The preacher gave me the answer: nobody … except Jesus."

Finally Mark had to speak up. "What are you trying to say, Sis, that no one but Jesus is going to be in heaven? That just doesn't make sense!" He was almost angry now.

"No, Mark," she said with a slight laugh. "But, I guess I am saying He's the only one that will be there because He deserves to be. All the rest will be there because of what Jesus did for them, not what they did to please God. You see, since everybody sins, nobody measures up to God's standards. And since God is God, He couldn't just forget about everyone's sin and let them in heaven. It's kind of like when we were little and Mom or Dad would spank us for something we did wrong. Well, God had to punish someone for our sins, so He decided to punish Jesus instead of punishing us in Hell."

"I'm sorry," Mark shook his head. "I'm just not following you. What are you getting at?"

"Mark, have you ever wondered why Jesus died on the cross?"

"No, not really. I just heard He did. I've never really given it much thought."

"Well, think about it now because it's important. Remember that time you were horsing around in the family room when you were about nine, and you bumped Mom's favorite lamp and broke it?"

"Sure I do," Mark replied with a confused look. "I guess I've always felt guilty about you taking the blame for me. You got that big lecture about carelessness and responsibility and then couldn't watch television for two weeks. You even had to work and earn the money to replace the lamp. I was a real jerk to let you take the blame. Why did you do it anyway?"

"Because I loved you, I guess. I can still see the horror in your face and the tears in your eyes as you looked at the broken lamp. I just couldn't stand the thought of you getting whipped. I figured I was too old for a spanking, so I decided to take my chances."

Mark still looked bewildered. "What's this got to do with our conversation, or are you just trying to change the subject?"

"Don't you see?" Katie labored. "That's what Jesus did for us on the cross. God punished Him for everyone else's sins. Jesus willingly took the blame for us."

Mark's expression brightened as if a light bulb went on in his head. Then that befuddled look resurfaced. "Wait a minute," he said slowly. "Are you saying that everyone is going to be in heaven?"

"No, Mark," Katie tried to be patient.

"But you said Jesus died for everyone's sins so they could go to heaven. Right?" he countered.

"Well, yes, I did say that. And having your sins forgiven is a free gift, but…." She paused as she once again measured her words. "I guess that's the best way to explain it. Going to heaven is a free gift, but it's not yours until you take it. About two weeks ago, I told Jesus that I wanted His gift … I wanted to have my sins forgiven … I wanted to have Jesus in my life."

"Well, what was His answer?" Mark said slightly sarcastically.

"He gave me that gift. He took away my guilt and became my friend. Something really did happen. I can't put it into words, but I really am different. God has helped me so much these last couple of weeks. Oh, Mark, I'm still scared of going up north and living with Lucas. Sometimes I think I can't go through with it, but then I remember that Jesus is with me now to help me and take care of me, and I know I'll make it somehow."

Katie had been looking down at her plate. When she looked up into her brother's eyes, she saw tears. "Forgive me, Katie," he murmured softly, "for getting you into this mess. I love you, Sis. I'm really gonna miss you. Please say you forgive me."

"I forgive you, Little Brother." Katie smiled through her tears. "And I love you a bunch."

CHAPTER 11

Sunday came quickly for Katie. Stepping out into the bright warm sunshine, she paused and looked around with a sigh. She would miss this place she'd called home for almost two years. So much had happened here.

Holding on to a feeling of excitement and expectancy tinged with melancholy, she treasured each moment as she attended Sunday School and the morning services. Then she went out to lunch with Patti and her friends one last time. They treated her to a dinner at a nicer than usual restaurant, and then each presented her with a special gift. Each young woman had chosen a Christian book that had helped her personally in her life. The pastor and his wife had heard about the plan and had sent along their own choices. The subjects varied. One was on prayer, another on joy, another on overcoming temptation. One was even on marriage. Each book was personally signed with a brief note so she could remember the giver. With obvious sincerity, each friend promised to pray for her.

Katie was inwardly overjoyed. The love and thoughtfulness of these new acquaintances touched her. She had known everyone, except Patti, for only two weeks, but they felt like old and trusted friends. She suddenly realized how much she would miss them and how much she needed to learn to become the kind of Christians these women were. Hopefully these books about God's Word would help.

That evening Mark showed up at church instead of dropping by afterwards to take her to the airport. She was hopeful. She could tell he was interested and curious, but unsure of what to think about all he heard.

Finally the time for good-byes came, first at the church, then at the airport. Mark watched with curious wonder as his sister appeared to treasure each new friend with one last teary embrace. Interwoven with the emotions of the moment, Katie silently questioned, "Will my future ever include other friendships like these?"

At the airport she could tell her brother's emotions included guilt. He hugged her tenderly as he whispered the now familiar words in her ear, "I'm so sorry for putting you in this position. Somehow I've got to make this up to you. I'm so sorry … so sorry …" Then his voice broke.

When Katie responded, she found her own voice shaky, too. "Remember, Mark. I told you that Jesus is my friend now, and He has promised to work all this out in my life. I'm still kind of afraid inside, but I'm going to trust Him to do what He promised." One last hug and she was walking to the airplane with only a brief look back.

During the flight she pondered her future as she looked out of the window at the glittering lights below. Some areas were well lit, but as the airplane climbed into the clouds she could see nothing. That's the way she felt about her life. She was in the middle of a dark cloud with no visible way out. As she began to discuss her feelings with God, she discovered a peculiar new feeling that had been surfacing lately. She had a strange inexplicable hope. She thought of the simple verse Patti had left her with, though Patti couldn't have known how very much she needed it.

"When I am afraid, I will trust in You."

She murmured the verse over and over as the airplane landed, as she walked down the ramp, and as she scanned the airport looking for her new husband.

"When I am afraid, I will trust in You."

She spotted him just as he saw her. Their eyes met. She forced a timid smile as she considered what she had seen in his look. Had there been anticipation, excitement maybe? Or had it only been recognition? She was afraid to hope for the best. She was fully aware that there was no love there.

"When I am afraid, I will trust in You."

Lucas was surprised at his own emotion. He reminded himself that this was only a business arrangement with additional personal benefits. He willed himself to remember that this innocent-looking, young woman would never worm her way into his affections because he never intended to make himself vulnerable to the kind of pain he had lived through the past few years.

"After all," he thought as he reined in his unexpected feelings. "Who wouldn't be excited to see the realization of a fantasy?" She was all that he remembered and more. Her new hairdo framed her face quite attractively. He thought she was even prettier than he remembered. Maybe it was the new outfit, too. All this went through his mind as he ushered her to the baggage claim and located her luggage.

The long automobile ride into the country was a quiet one, but both parties were coming to expect that. Lucas preferred to immerse himself in his thoughts and not be distracted by chatter. For Katie, the silence was growing more comfortable. At least during these times she didn't have to worry about saying the wrong thing.

As the car slowed to turn off onto a paved driveway, Katie glanced briefly at Lucas. Though his stalwart expression didn't reveal it, she sensed his anticipation. In the darkness, the driveway seemed engulfed by large tree branches. Katie felt as if her world was in slow motion as the car slowly followed the bending lane toward her new life. As Lucas rounded the final turn in the lane, it was his turn to view his new wife's reaction. Up ahead stood his beautiful home, nestled in the protective arms of at least a dozen mature trees. Expertly placed spotlights displayed the beauty and grace of the building. The lighting had been done for the purpose of security, but Lucas had been proud of the impressive look it gave the property. He was pleased with the quick intake of breath he heard from the other side of the car. He knew she was impressed.

Katie had assumed that a man able to pay what he did for her services as wife would live in a nice house, yet she had not expected this. The home was not a mansion, but it was large. It was two stories high with a porch extending across the front. The word elegant came to her mind at this first glimpse.

Lucas purposely brought her in the front door to make an impression, instead of parking in the garage and going in through the kitchen. The first thing she saw as she stepped into the spacious entryway was a large winding staircase with a beautiful chandelier hanging from the ceiling at the top. To her right was a huge great room with a cathedral ceiling and a large impressive fireplace at the end. She felt as if she'd walked into a magazine, displaying the perfect house. The effective blend of colors with furnishings that would undoubtedly earn the approval of society's most respected home decorators awed her, yet left her cold. The immaculate room was devoid of warmth, looking very unlived in.

Lucas knew Katie was probably very tired, and he should forego a tour of the house tonight, but he wanted to watch her as she got a glimpse of each room. He would have to leave early tomorrow morning for work. So he followed his desires and began to show her each room. At the far end of the living room was an entrance to a large formal dining room that led into a sun room. The dining room also exited into a den and the kitchen. The large country kitchen also had an entrance through the alcove underneath the winding staircase.

Beyond the entranceway, they peeked into a roomy laundry which included a folding and ironing area. Passing two doors Lucas described as storage areas, they came to two large bedrooms with a bath in between. Once back at the entryway, they came to a door that led to a smaller staircase which wound downward. At the bottom she found herself in a huge game room stocked with ping pong, billiards, and table hockey. She could even see an enclosed area with a variety of what was obviously the latest in weight room equipment. To the far right, she noticed a kitchenette which included a refrigerator, a microwave, and cabinets. Three bar stools lined the dividing counter. Several comfortable chairs, each with a table and lamp at the side, were placed along the walls. In the left hand corner there was a small cozy-looking den with a fireplace.

Katie followed Lucas up the stairs in silence. She had attempted polite comments as she viewed each room, but she worried that everything she said sounded lame and inappropriate. Lucas picked up her suitcases then started up the wide impressive staircase to the upper floor. At the top Katie faced two large oak panels which appeared to slide open for entrance. Lucas nodded his head in that direction and said, "… library of sorts …" He slid the heavy door open a few inches for her perusal of the room. At a glance she noticed the walls lined with bookcases of dark cherry wood. A small desk of the same wood was to her left with several comfortable chairs and a small couch placed tastefully around the room.

Then without another word he went to the right and carried her luggage past a large bathroom and into a bedroom. As Katie stepped through the door she marveled once again at the decorative charm. She was in the sitting area of a large, exquisitely-designed bedroom with obviously feminine décor.

"You can put all your belongings in here," Lucas was saying. "In fact, you might as well just stay in here tonight since it's so late, and I have to get up early tomorrow. My bedroom is at the end of the hall. After tonight you'll sleep in there. You can see it in the morning."

"Are you hungry?" he changed the subject abruptly.

"No," she murmured, "I had a snack on the plane."

"Good," came the reply. "Now here's what I want you to do tomorrow. As you can see, the place won't need cleaning yet, and don't worry about my breakfast in the morning. Sleep late if you want, but when you do get up, I want you to spend the day getting organized. Make a list of everything you will need to do to keep my house in its present condition. Also, make a list of the cleaning supplies you prefer.

"In addition to that, I want you to write down menus of future meals. Tomorrow when I get home, we'll go over these lists and I'll make suggestions."

When Lucas paused, Katie spoke up. "What would you like for supper tomorrow evening?"

"Don't worry about that. I'm not sure what food I have down there right now. We'll go out tomorrow night, and then we'll stop by the grocery on the way home to pick up what you need. I want to get you out where you can be seen anyway, so the word will get around that I have a new bride." Lucas appeared pleased with this idea.

"I'll be home about six tomorrow evening. You get some rest now, Katlyn. You look like you need it."

With that less than complimentary comment, Lucas left the room, closing the door behind him. Katie couldn't help letting a sigh of relief escape. She was so grateful for a little solitude on this first night. She breathed a prayer of thanks as she gazed around the room.

This room, like the rest of the house, was done in a stylish decor in the latest colors. The effect was somewhat breathtaking, yet the perfection around her seemed almost unfriendly. She wondered if the house could ever feel like home. As she sat on the king-sized bed, she also wondered if she could keep this huge house in the immaculate condition it was in at the present.

Just then a thought came to her. She had her friend Jesus to help. He would show her how to do it. With that comfort she dressed for bed, spent a few moments reading her Bible, and went to sleep after saying goodnight to her Lord.

Lucas went to his room after turning out all the lights in the house. He was pleased with himself. He was positive he had been right about spending a small fortune to have a housekeeping service come in and clean his home to perfection. He'd paid all sorts of extra fees to have them do jobs not normally included, but he wanted every nook and cranny spotless. This woman needed to see how he expected her to keep his domain. No one else had ever done that before, certainly not Adrian. Some of the housekeepers had been better than others, but none were hardworking enough to keep it like this. It was going to be different this time. He would start out firm and keep on this woman till she got it right. After all she couldn't give him her two weeks notice if she didn't like him.

As he drifted off to sleep, Lucas was reliving moments of the tour of his house, remembering Katie's expressions as she moved from one room to another. But the dreams were altered as another face began to appear in each room. This second face was very beautiful, but filled his night with bitterness and hatred. He awoke unrested and in a dark mood … angry that Adrian was still able to poison his existence. Would he ever have any peace again?

CHAPTER 12

Katie woke early, but she moved around quietly in her bedroom until she heard the sound of the garage door opening and closing, then the fading hum of tires down the driveway. She just didn't feel like facing her husband if it wasn't necessary. After a brief inventory of the kitchen, she was grateful she didn't have to make supper tonight. The pantry shelves were spotless, but they were also almost empty. All she could manage for breakfast was some toast and coffee.

She was actually eager to begin her private assessment of her new responsibilities, but she knew she would need some spiritual nourishment, too, so she spent some time in her Bible and prayer before she started her task. Patti had encouraged her to spend time with God. According to her friend it was essential. She found a pad of paper and a pen up in the room Lucas referred to as the library then tried to decide just where to begin. Since she was already upstairs, she started with the bedroom in which Lucas had deposited all her belongings. She would have to unpack later once she had completed the assignments Lucas had given her.

She listed each room and wrote down everything she could think of that would need to be done to keep it in perfect condition. In the margin she listed any cleaning supplies she would need to get the job done. After she inspected the library, she moved down the hall to Lucas' room. She was not surprised to find it as large as the one she had slept in the night before. It also included a mammoth bath and a sitting area. The room almost looked like a mini apartment. What did astonish her was that this room actually looked lived in. The bed was unmade; clothes were not put away, and the bathroom was clean but not spotless. She perceived that Lucas was not quite the neat freak he had appeared to be. Relief flooded Katie. She left the room after adding to her list and making a note to return and clean this room before Lucas returned home.

She made another welcome discovery upon leaving the bedroom. A door immediately across from his door led to a small office. Katie was pleased to see it was equipped with a computer and printer.

"Thank you, Lord," she murmured. "This will help me get organized."

The working tour of the house took most of the morning. She also took note of what cleaning supplies she found. There was very little. It was obvious that Lucas did not do his own cleaning.

Katie managed to find a little something for lunch which she took into the sun room beyond the dining room. While she munched on her meal, she took in the scenery behind the house, marveling at the beauty of the property. To her left as far as she could see, she noticed woods with thick undergrowth. Directly behind the house was a large, neatly-manicured lawn. Beyond the yard to the right seemed to be a pasture bordered by another clump of woods. She could just make out a quaint wooden bridge over the stream that went through both meadow and woods. She could not imagine a more idyllic setting. She wondered how much of this acreage belonged to Lucas.

A sudden urge to go exploring came over her, but she had to resist. Hopefully she would find the time to do that soon, but this afternoon there was just too much to do. With that thought she hurriedly cleaned up her small mess and considered where to go to bring some organization to her many lists.

Her decision led her down to the basement back in the corner. Of all the rooms in the house, this one felt the coziest. She plopped down on a small overstuffed couch. Spreading out all her sheets of paper in front of her, she began to sort through all the jobs, transferring each to new lists. There were things to be done daily, every other day, weekly, semi-weekly, monthly, and bimonthly.

When she was satisfied with her choices, she turned to the problem of supplies. Her final list concerned the suggested menus for a week. This was really difficult. Other than the one day she had spent with her new husband when they married, she hadn't the slightest notion what foods he liked. So in addition to the menus, she listed many varieties of foods to ask him what his preferences were.

Once her brainwork was complete, she ascended two flights of stairs to the little office across from Lucas' room. In no time at all, she had all her work neatly organized, typed, printed, and waiting for approval. She was pleased with herself. She honestly felt as if she'd put forth her best work, and that it was a job well done. It was about 2:45 so she began to bring Lucas' bedroom back into shape to match the rest of the house. She was sure she'd have plenty of time to clean it and then get ready for his return at six.

She started by taking his dirty clothes downstairs and putting in a load of wash. She was glad he at least had laundry products. Next she tried to put the room in order without really knowing where to put things. This took some time because she had to snoop to find places for everything. Finally after putting the wet clothes in the dryer and starting another load, she began on Lucas' bathroom. As she worked she thanked God for the wisdom and help He had given so far and asked Him for help to face whatever might come her way here in this house.

She nearly jumped out of her skin when she suddenly heard Lucas' angry voice speaking. "Katlyn, what do you think you are doing?"

Looking up with surprise and confusion she replied, "I'm cleaning this bathtub."

"I can see that! What I want to know is why you are doing that when I told you explicitly to be doing something else today?" he spit out fiercely.

Katie carefully searched his eyes, then stood without speaking, and walked deliberately out of the bathroom and out of the bedroom. Lucas watched as she crossed the hall to the office. Picking up a small stack of papers, she carried them back and handed them to the speechless man, knelt back down on the floor, and went back to her work.

Lucas' mind raced as he quickly looked over the neatly organized pages laying out the housework exactly as he had wanted ... only better. Then he scanned the menus, unable to find fault with them as well. This wasn't going at all as he had planned. From the moment he left the house this morning, Lucas' mind had been devising a scheme to lay the correct foundation for this relationship. He felt a need to establish his superior position in this arrangement. As the morning proceeded, he couldn't keep his mind on his own work. He kept wondering what Katie was doing and imagining how things would be when he returned home. He envisioned coming home to find an average job done that he could pick apart to show this young wife who was the boss.

His distraction was so complete; he had managed to accomplish absolutely no work. Instead of being apologetic to his coworkers for his failure, he became irritable, blaming the new employee in the office because she hadn't read his mind and finished the job he forgot to ask her to do. Thoroughly frustrated, he had thrown some papers in a briefcase and started for home almost two hours early. Forgetting the premature time, he was now infuriated to find Katie cleaning instead of organizing the housework. "How dare she ignore his orders on the very first day?" his mind had shouted in silent indignation.

Now as the sickening truth of the situation washed over him, his brain struggled to comprehend. Katie had exceeded his expectations and still found time to go beyond what he asked … to do more. He couldn't let her win, though … not now, right at the start. He must establish his supremacy.

In a low growling voice he started. "This doesn't explain what you are doing now. I expressly told you not to work on the house today. You must learn to do exactly what I say. I told you we were going out tonight for dinner. Are you planning on wearing jeans? Why aren't you ready?"

Katie had not turned to face him during this little tirade. She had been frozen in disbelief, her hand still holding the sponge against the side of the tub. She slowly turned, but not to face Lucas … to look at the clock. Lucas followed her gaze and saw that it was 4:22 in the afternoon. He was wrong again. He had told her he would be home at six. As he struggled for words, Katie stood suddenly leaving the tub unfinished as she turned to leave the room.

"Just where are you going now?" he sputtered.

"To get ready for dinner," she answered softly as she passed through the door. Lucas fully expected to hear the bedroom door slam behind her, but it did not. She didn't slam it, but he was afraid he could read her mood in the way she closed it firmly.

"Oh, brother," he muttered to himself. "Now I'm in trouble." He had really looked forward to this evening. In his morning reverie he had pictured the scene so clearly. After adequately putting Katie in her place by changing and reorganizing her cleaning schedule, they would go out for a relaxing evening at one of the restaurants he frequented.

This would successfully advertise his new wife to anyone who might recognize him. Now after this, she was sure to be moody and out of sorts. Maybe he should just order a pizza and forget going out. He glanced briefly at her bedroom door as he went downstairs to ponder his options.

Katie was indeed upset when she firmly shut the bedroom door behind her. How could this have happened? She had been praying all day about this evening. Why didn't God answer her prayers? It just didn't seem fair!

As Katie's eyes dropped, she saw her Bible on the table in the sitting area. She sat down and opened it where she had marked the place she had been reading this morning. A devotional book Patti had given her had taken her to II Corinthians 12. She didn't understand exactly what the verses meant, but she could tell that Paul had asked God to take away some problem three times, but God hadn't done it. Instead the Lord told him that God's grace was sufficient, and God's power was perfected in Paul's weakness. All this hadn't meant a whole lot this morning, but right now it was ringing true. Katie wanted God to take away her problems, but evidently He wasn't going to do that this time.

"Lord," she said quietly, "I guess You're not going to fix everything, so I really need this grace You're talking about here ... whatever that is. I'm a prime candidate for Your strength because right now I definitely feel my weakness. All I can say is, 'help!' I can't do this myself."

With that prayer on her lips, Katie hurriedly dressed for dinner. As she walked downstairs to find her husband, she realized that her heart was lighter. The anger had subsided. She had a peace she had not expected. She also noticed there was music playing all over the house.

Lucas had turned on the music, hoping to clear the air a little. He had installed a stereo system that could be turned on or off in every room of the house. He had switched on his favorite station, one that played "oldies." His back was to the door so he heard Katie come in before he saw her. He dreaded the sober face he was sure to see when he turned, so he spoke instead of looking.

"Come over and sit down so we can talk about your plans here," he said as he fingered the pages. "It's still a little early for dinner."

Katie smiled slightly as she considered how impatient Lucas had been when she wasn't ready yet. And now it's too early for dinner? The smile lingered long enough for Lucas to notice it as she seated herself beside him. Relief washed over him as he noted Katie's countenance. There was no trace of the dark mood he had expected. In fact, it felt as if a breath of fresh air had entered the room.

Katie broke the silence. "I hope my outfit is appropriate. I wasn't sure where we were going for dinner."

"Perfect," Lucas responded immediately. He hadn't been trying to be complimentary. He was honestly impressed with her casual yet feminine look.

The ice had been broken, so he plunged on. "I've been looking over your organization of the housework, and I think you have a handle on things. You will probably find you need to do some adjusting as you begin to actually do the work. The dusting, for instance, won't be necessary as often as you expect. I've installed a top-of-the-line air filtration system, so there is very little dust in the house."

"That's wonderful," Katie answered sincerely. "And I can easily make scheduling changes on the computer; that is, as long as you don't mind my using your computer."

"Well, I am somewhat concerned that you might inadvertently delete some important financial information. Are you sure you know enough about computers to use it safely?" Lucas said with genuine concern.

"Quite sure," she replied, stifling a chuckle. "I took a business course after high school. Computers I can handle."

Satisfied, Lucas broached the next subject. "The menu for next week looks fine, but what is this other list of foods? Not a grocery list I hope!"

"No, no, no!" Katie spoke hurriedly. "I just wanted you to go through the list and tell me your likes and dislikes, so I have a better idea of what to fix."

Lucas made no reply. Katie felt uncomfortable until she realized he was reading through the list, marking certain foods out and making notes by others. Katie tried to relax by listening to the music to relax but to no avail. She felt so out of place. She soon forgot the music and began to pray.

"Please help, Lord. I can't do this. You've got to help!" As Katie continued her prayer, she unconsciously closed her eyes.

"Katlyn!" the sudden voice startled her. "Are you going to sleep?"

"Oh, no," she answered meekly. "I just had my eyes closed."

He gave her a curious look then continued marking her list. Finally he looked up abruptly. "Do you have a grocery list made out yet?"

"Yes," she said quietly, not knowing if this was the answer he wanted or not.

"All right," he responded with no particular expression. "I'm going up to change for dinner."

An hour later they were ordering at one of the nicer family restaurants in the area. Just as Lucas had hoped, they were noticed by some of his acquaintances. When friends stopped by their table and were introduced, Lucas was charming and witty, but as soon as they were alone he was back to his aloof demeanor. He was distant and cool until someone new passed by to say hello.

At the grocery store he pushed the cart silently as she found the items she had put on her list for this week's menu, as well as all the cleaning supplies she needed. Occasionally, he would stop suddenly and take some food item off the shelf, consider it briefly, and then put it either in the cart or back on the shelf. All this was done without a word of comment.

She would have preferred some advice as far as his preferences, but it was apparent that she would have no help from him. She suspected this was a test, and she had no idea if she was passing or failing.

Her heart pounded as the cashier passed each item through the computerized check out. She knew the final bill was going to be substantial, but she hoped Lucas would understand that he was out of almost everything. When the total was given, she smothered a gasp, but her husband offered his credit card to the clerk as if this were perfectly normal. She wondered if this was an act, and he would explode as soon as they reached the car, but he seemed totally unbothered.

Halfway home she was so tired of his cool silence, she almost thought she would have preferred a heated confrontation.

"I'm sorry you had to pay so much for the groceries," she finally blurted out.

"It wasn't that much," he replied unemotionally. Those were the only words spoken during the trip home. When they arrived, he carried all the groceries into the kitchen. Before he left the room, he spoke. "Come up to my room when you've finished putting everything away. You'll be sleeping in there from now on, but you can leave your clothes and belongings in the other bedroom. It will give us both more room. Breakfast will need to be ready by seven." Then he was gone.

Later that night Katie lay awake beside her sleeping husband wondering how long she could stand their strange relationship. She was so close to him, and yet she felt so very far away. She went over and over the evening in her mind, trying to decide if she should have done anything differently. She came to the conclusion that maybe she should have, but she didn't have the slightest idea in what way. She found herself crying out again for God's help to go through another day. As her pastor's wife had encouraged her, she would just have to make a choice to believe that God would help. Her own feelings right now were telling her the situation was hopeless. With those mixed emotions, she finally drifted off to sleep.

CHAPTER 13

The next few days were uncomfortable for both Lucas and Katie. Neither was sure how to act in the new positions. Lucas had spent four years in solitude, developing a deep bitterness toward women. He came into this situation with a solid determination that this woman would never touch him emotionally. At the same time, he found it refreshing to have another human being around. He found himself thinking about her when he was away, wondering what she was doing, sometimes even wondering what she was thinking. He saw an innocence in her that he had not expected in this unusual arrangement. He tried to remind himself that she couldn't be so innocent and have gotten herself in such a bind, but what he saw in her just didn't match up.

Sometimes Lucas would slip into an almost friendly attitude though never really warm. Then when he realized he was softening toward his young bride, he would suddenly become cold and force himself to be uncaring. Then he would congratulate himself for not being trapped in the spider's web.

Meanwhile, Katie had no idea what was going on in Lucas' mind. At first she felt herself responding to him when he appeared to be warming up to her, but after a couple of times of being rewarded with a sudden wall of ice between them, she learned to protect her own feelings in self-defense.

In this first week they initiated a sort of employer/ employee relationship that could develop without danger to either one's emotional well-being. During the day while Lucas was at work, Katie could relax and enjoy taking care of the beautiful home, even if it didn't feel like her own. In the evening she was pleasant but distant since that seemed to be what Lucas demanded.

She found the controls for the stereo system in the library and began to fill the house with music during the day. She discovered a Christian radio station that not only played uplifting Christian music but also had a variety of sermons throughout the day. As a newborn baby Christian she soaked everything in, sometimes stopping in the middle of a task to run and get her Bible to see if it really said what the preacher claimed. Each day passed quickly with these invisible companions.

On Wednesday of that first week, Lucas suddenly got an idea to check and see if Katie was loafing all day or actually working. He told his secretary he had a luncheon appointment and would be gone for a couple of hours and started for home. When he reached the house, he stepped quietly in the door and was surprised to find music permeating the air. He walked stealthily from one room to another, hoping to see Katie before she saw him. As he left the kitchen and was about to make his way up the staircase, he noticed that the washer was going in the laundry room. The door was slightly ajar so he could peek in without being noticed. Sure enough there was Katie, ironing one of his shirts as she hummed along with the music. He stood there motionless, taking in her every move. She was so much more at ease than she was in the evenings when he was at home. She seemed happier than he had ever seen her.

Momentarily, he felt guilt attempt to raise its head and accuse him of wrong in trapping this pretty young girl in this loveless relationship. Immediately he squelched such ideas, replacing them with thoughts of how grateful this girl should be to share such a beautiful house with him. After a few more moments watching, Lucas slipped away unnoticed and went back to work, satisfied that his wife was not lazy … at least not today. Maybe he would try this again soon.

On Friday evening Lucas announced that they would be playing tennis with friends on Sunday afternoon. He noticed Katie's disconcerted look and asked, "You do play tennis, don't you?"

"Only with my younger brother," she answered, "and that was years ago."

"Well, we'll just have to go out tomorrow and see what you can do. I don't want to be embarrassed in front of Tom and Amy," he said stiffly. "We've got the whole day to work on it. We'll go out right after breakfast tomorrow morning."

"I'll do my best," Katie mumbled, not really sure that would be enough.

Then came another of the frequent silent periods that occurred when they were together. Katie was searching for the right words to ask something she had been trying to bring up most of the week. Finally she broke the silence.

"Is there any way I could go to church Sunday morning? I could be back in plenty of time for tennis with your friends."

"No!" his blunt reply hit her like a bullet.

"But why not?" her words tumbled out.

"Because I said so. I don't want a bunch of hypocrites coming to my door asking for handouts for some stuffy church," he shot back.

"But, I …" Katie started.

"I said no, Katlyn, and there will be no more discussion on the subject," Lucas responded icily.

Katie was silenced as well as devastated. She had so looked forward to finding a church and gaining Christian friends like Patti and those she had left just a week ago.

All she could think was that here was another impossible request to include in her prayer journal. She wondered when she could start writing in some answers to prayer, but she wouldn't give up hope yet. God would answer. He must!

CHAPTER 14

The tennis practice on Saturday proved to be better than Lucas had expected. Katie was thankful that Mark had gone out for the tennis team in high school and had begged his big sister to play with him so he could improve his game. Lucas was surprised at her coordination. He hadn't played for some time himself, so it was good for him to get back into form. He'd been pretty good in college. Then after he and Adrian had gotten together, they had made a great team. Since Adrian's death, he'd only been on the court a couple of times.

With Katie here, he had a reason to play again. It was all part of his advertising to certain people that he had a wife. So when his old friend Tom Stone suggested a game of doubles, Lucas jumped at the idea. Lucas explained all this to Katie as they ate lunch out after their tennis practice. He also revealed that Tom was also his doctor and that his wife, Amy, worked in Lucas' office. He had met Tom at an office party, and they had immediately become close friends. Lucas was aware that Dr. Tom had been concerned about him as he watched the change in him after Adrian's death. He was hoping this would reassure the physician that all was well again. At the same time, other acquaintances would see him with Katie and pass the word that he was now happily remarried.

The next day proved to be a perfect spring day. Katie once again pondered her new life as she watched the sun come up through the bedroom window. As the shadows gave way to sunlight, she glanced at the face of her sleeping husband. Could it be that she had been here only one week? In some ways that week had seemed like an eternity. True, her days were going a little more smoothly as she seemed to be developing a routine. Yet this handsome man beside her was still such a stranger. At this moment she honestly wondered if it would ever be any different. She squeezed her eyelids together as if in doing so she could shut out such thoughts. Then she lifted her heart to God in silent prayer, repeating the words she had said so many times this week.

"Lord, please work this out for good as you promised. Help me to be patient until you do. I'm still having trouble believing you can do anything with this mess, so I'm just going to choose to believe You, even if I don't feel like it.

"I wish I could go to church. These last few Sundays have meant so much to me. Patti and the other people at her church seem almost like a family, and I really miss them. I do thank You for showing me that Christian radio station. I think I've learned something new from the Bible every day, and listening to the music and preaching while I work has helped so much. I still feel as if I need to be in church, Lord, yet what can I do? If Lucas won't let me, what choice do I have? Please work it out so I can go soon, and maybe even work it out for Lucas to go with me some day."

As the thought popped into her head, she glanced over at the sleeping figure beside her. She had to admit that the idea of Lucas going to church seemed out of the realm of possibility.

"Well, Lord, I guess that's just one more of those impossible things I'll leave with You. I can't even imagine that happening.

"And now, Lord, about this tennis outing today. I'm really afraid. I don't know how to act. Lucas wants everyone to think we're a happily married couple when in reality we rarely talk to each other. We share a bed; yet we're little more than strangers. Please, Lord, I really need your help."

At this point, Lucas stirred beside her so she decided to slip out of bed and read her Bible before he woke up. She tiptoed into the library and curled up in an overstuffed chair with God's Word. This time was so refreshing. She didn't understand a lot of what she read, but every day some verse seemed to have special meaning just for her that moment.

She was so focused on the verses she was reading she didn't notice Lucas standing in the doorway watching. As she paused a moment, she glanced up to catch an unreadable look in his eye. Katie was so startled she jumped up immediately, letting her Bible fall to the floor.

"Oh, you're up. Are you ready for some breakfast?" she blurted out quickly. She felt awkward and uncomfortable because Lucas had caught her not working. Her mind assured her that he didn't expect her to work every waking moment seven days a week, but somehow her body couldn't relax in his presence if she wasn't busy with some task.

Lucas read her awkwardness immediately. He was pleased he could read her expressions as well as he had hoped, but he didn't feel good about her obvious discomfort in his presence. He had been standing at the door for some time enjoying the peaceful scene. She had looked so serene as she studied the pages intently with her tousled hair in her soft silk nightie. He hadn't noticed what she was reading until her Bible fell to the floor with a thud when he startled her. Now he almost felt as if he had committed a sin by intruding at a sacred moment, but he quickly brushed those thoughts aside.

After a brief but awkward silence, he replied, "Let's just have some coffee and toast now. We can eat an early lunch so we won't be playing tennis with a full stomach."

"Sure, as soon as I'm dressed," she answered quickly.

"You don't have to get all dressed up to drink coffee with your husband. You do drink coffee, don't you?"

"Yes, I do," she said meekly.

"Then go make us some." Lucas replied firmly, but his insistence came with a half smile which softened the order.

As Lucas watched Katie disappear down the stairway, he wondered at his own words. When he had awakened to find Katie missing, curiosity had been his motive in finding her. He'd had no intention of sharing breakfast with her. All week, after fixing his breakfast, she had busied herself with cleaning up, letting her husband eat in solitude as he read the morning paper. Seeing Katie in the library looking so winsome and cozy had put him in the mood for her company.

As he walked back into his bedroom, he spotted the bottle of cologne sitting on his dresser. He had made it a point to leave it out as a constant reminder. Yes, a reminder that he must never again be humiliated by the betrayal of a woman. As he pondered the small travel-sized bottle, the warm feeling he had earlier dissolved. As he walked slowly down the circular staircase, he renewed his resolution to bar emotions from this marriage.

When he walked into the kitchen, Katie noticed the chill in his disposition ... so different from his attitude only minutes ago. She wondered what she had done to antagonize him. She retreated into her shell to protect her feelings from new disappointment.

The breakfast for two was quiet and awkward. In fact the whole morning was uncomfortable. With Lucas home she didn't know what to do with herself. She had scheduled no particular tasks to be done since it was Sunday, but she had a nagging feeling that her husband expected her to be doing something productive.

In reality Lucas didn't care what she did. He was more than satisfied with her performance this week though he had not bothered to say anything. He had come home to check on her three times this week. It was easy to move about the house unheard since Katie always utilized the stereo system with the speaker turned on in every room. The second trip home had almost convinced him that she was lounging instead of laboring. He had searched the entire house, finding no sign of her. He had looked around outside then came back in for a second look around. By this time he was fuming but also getting slightly concerned that she might have left him for good.

After searching the main floor and upstairs again, he nervously descended the stairs to the basement for one last look. Walking halfway into the game room, he glanced in every direction, thinking he had missed nothing. Just as he was about to make his way back up the stairs, he heard a voice coming from the small den in the corner. He quietly stepped closer and stopped suddenly when he saw a busy figure cleaning the ashes out of the fireplace.

She looked so cute with smudges of ash on her nose and cheek that he wanted to go in and speak to her. Yet he had no explanation for his presence there in the middle of the day, so he just stood outside the door watching her work. As on previous occasions, she was humming along with the music, looking happier than she ever did when he was around. When his conscience threatened his peaceful attitude, he left quickly and returned to the office.

On his third attempt to "check on her," he found her on her hand and knees washing the kitchen floor. After this he never worried about her working. She wasn't lazy. He needn't watch to make sure the work was done. She had earned his respect in that area. His home had never been cleaner. He expected no work at all from her this day other than a couple of meals, but it never crossed his mind to tell her. He thoughtlessly assumed she would understand this fact.

Later at the tennis outing Lucas discovered some other expectations he shouldn't have assumed. After they arrived at the country club and introductions were made, Lucas thought Katie would immediately fall into character as a socialite wife, but he soon saw that she had never lived in his world. Amy kept talking about stores and fashion designers that Katie seemed to have never heard of, or at least she had no great interest in them. He had supposed that since Adrian and Amy had been close and he and Tom were best friends that, of course, Katie would just fit right in ... but it was obvious that she didn't.

Then came the giant blunder. Amy, seeing that she was getting nowhere talking fashion and social functions, changed the subject to one she felt sure would be well received.

She began in her bubbly way, "Oh, Katlyn, I'm sure you just can't wait to go with Lucas on his business trip to Hawaii!"

Katie immediately looked to Lucas and saw panic in his eyes. At the same moment her heart leaped. She had always dreamed of going to Hawaii.

As Katie's mind raced for a reply that was safe, Amy continued babbling, unaware of the discomfort she was causing. "Tom and I are looking forward to it, even though this will be our third journey to the islands. You just can't get enough of the gorgeous blue water, the white sand beaches, the native dances, or the luscious food no matter how often you go. I know Lucas has been there before. How about you, Katlyn? Will this be your first visit?"

"Well, uh, I've never been to Hawaii," Katie stumbled, looking to her husband for help.

"Amy, didn't Tom tell you that Katlyn won't be joining us for this trip. We thought it might ruin our plans to go to Hawaii for our belated honeymoon," Lucas filled in quickly.

Katie's heart sank as Amy continued. "Oh, that's too bad. It would be so much fun! Katlyn and I could really get to know each other quickly in perfect surroundings like that. Do change your minds," Amy whined with an artificial pout on her face.

"Well, I'm sure you girls can find some other way to get better acquainted," Lucas added, lamely thinking at the same time that he wanted to keep Katie away from Amy for awhile. He was beginning to fear that she might figure out that theirs was not a normal marriage.

The idea of spending much time with Amy made Katie increasingly uncomfortable. Her first impression of the young woman was that she was very shallow and superficial. This view of Dr. Tom's wife didn't change as the afternoon wore on; indeed, it seemed to intensify.

The contrast between the two women became more pronounced to Lucas throughout the afternoon, also. As the tennis ball was volleyed back and forth on the court, Lucas found himself mentally defending his new wife. "Maybe she isn't the most sophisticated woman in the world, and maybe she's never heard of the leading fashion designers of the day, but she has far more important and deeper qualities than that. She can … she's … she …"

Suddenly he had to admit that he didn't know what qualities his wife had. He didn't really know her at all. As he watched her bravely try to be whatever he wanted her to be, an intense desire welled up within him to really get to know her … to find out what makes her think and react as she does. But could he do that without getting emotionally involved? Right at this moment he felt as if it was worth a try. Maybe if he was very careful, they could develop an intellectual relationship without the romantic baggage. He'd think this one through later.

The ride home was quiet as usual until they were almost home. Lucas finally broke the silence.

"I guess I learned something today."

Katie turned to listen.

"If you're going to be seen with me in public, which of course is part of the plan, I'm going to have to give you more background information so you'll know how to respond. Today just reinforced my decision not to take you to Hawaii with me. There's no way you could hold up for two whole weeks among my business associates without someone becoming suspicious. It will be hard enough to fool Old Man Barnes and his wife when we go to dinner and a ballgame with them after the trip.

"And as far as that honeymoon business, I'll just have to make up some excuse for canceling that later. We'll just take one problem at a time for now."

Lucas paused, and Katie tried desperately to rein in her emotions. She had hoped maybe the honeymoon in Hawaii was for real, but now she saw it was just part of the cover. She was glad she hadn't known. She didn't feel as if she had lied to anyone because she hadn't understood the truth.

Taking a deep breath, Katie attempted to continue the conversation. "When will you be leaving for Hawaii?" she asked quietly.

"Three weeks from today," Lucas answered without hesitation. After several minutes of silence, Lucas spoke again. "Do you drive?"

"Yes, I do," replied Katie wondering what he was thinking.

"Good," he said. "When I leave for Hawaii, you can drop me off at O'Hare. Then you'll have the car for the two weeks so you can go to the store or whatever you need to do while I'm gone. Since you won't have as much to do without me around, you can have a vacation of sorts, too. Do whatever you want."

Lucas smiled to himself for being so benevolent as to offer his wife some time off while he basked in the sun on some island beach.

"Oh well," Katie thought. "It will be nice to spend some time alone."

Suddenly a new thought brightened her whole being. Lucas said she could do whatever she wanted. That meant she could go to church. She really hoped she could find one like the church she had left behind. It was something to look forward to anyway. She wouldn't mention this to Lucas. She didn't want to give him the chance to tell her she couldn't go.

CHAPTER 15

The next three weeks brought some adjustments in the Lehman house. Lucas and Katie were becoming accustomed to each other's presence. Though Katie still felt ill at ease around her husband when she was not busy, she felt more confidence in his satisfaction with her work. Lucas tried a couple of times to find fault with some completed task just to "show her who was boss," but finally dropped the notion. She seemed to make no mistakes. The house was immaculate; the meals were tasty and on time, and his wardrobe was always clean and pressed.

One fact was just beyond the man's conscious thought. Lucas enjoyed coming home for the first time in years. He had convinced himself after Adrian's death that he was a solitary kind of guy who enjoyed his privacy. He turned down many kind invitations from friends and co-workers, excusing his conscience with the idea that he wasn't a people person; he was a loner. The truth was that as much as he dreaded being around other people, he hated going home to an empty house full of memories even more. Some evenings he had taken long drives in the country just to put off going home to this solitude.

Life was different since Katie came to live with him. He never stopped to analyze the difference, but he definitely looked forward to seeing her each evening. She didn't talk much. Of course, that was part of the agreement she had signed when she married him. Yet even when she didn't say a word, her presence seemed somehow to be soothing. At times when he was in the mood for conversation, he regretted ever cautioning her to not talk too much. At least he had someone who would listen to him. He couldn't help wondering how much she really cared about the activities at the station he related to her. She acted interested anyway. That was more than Adrian had ever done. She never seemed to be interested in much other than herself and her own personal affairs.

All of this meant that Lucas had seriously considered finding some excuse to stay home instead of going to Hawaii. He really didn't look forward to spending two weeks across the ocean, but every excuse he thought of was so flimsy, he gave up the idea.

Unlike Lucas, Katie was really excited about her upcoming "vacation". She had pondered what she could do during that time. One treat would be that she could spend a lot of time reading the books Patti and her church friends had given her. She also wanted to spend lots of time outdoors exploring the acres that belonged to her husband. The day finally came for the drive to the airport. Before they left the house, Lucas gave detailed directions for Katie's return from O'Hare. She tried not to look impatient as he explained for the fourth time the exact route she should take. Finally, Lucas drove to the drop off point, reached for his suitcases, cautioned Katie to drive carefully in the Chicago traffic, then disappeared into the building with a quick goodbye.

Katie called after him, "Have a nice trip," but she wasn't sure he heard.

As Katie left the airport, she began to appreciate her husband's attention to detail. Even on a Sunday afternoon the streets of Chicago brought a new driving experience Katie never anticipated. Lucas had directed her by the Botanical Gardens, thinking she would like to browse before she returned home. Instead Katie had her mind on the first goal of her "vacation". She wanted to find a church to attend that night. After a considerable amount of driving around looking for one, she decided to go home and try the yellow pages. As little as she knew the area, she was sure she could get hopelessly lost. The first church she called responded with an answering machine giving the times of their services, but she had no idea where it was located. The second number she called reached a real person, but this church had no evening service. After a few more unsuccessful calls, she noticed a church that included service times in the listing. The street named in the address was familiar. She decided to get an early start and hope she could find it.

Katie arrived at the church in plenty of time, but she almost left immediately. The church was huge — much bigger than any she had ever attended in the past. Though this intimidated her, she decided she was unfair to reject it for this reason alone. She waited in her car until others were arriving and went through the door they were entering hoping she looked inconspicuous. When she entered the building, she realized not everyone was going to the same room. People seemed friendly enough, but they all seemed to be interested in their own friends or on what they had to accomplish before the service.

After pausing for an uncomfortable moment, she perceived that children were going in one general direction, teens in another, and most adults in a third. She proceeded in the third direction, hoping she looked as if she knew what she was doing. Once in the large auditorium, she found a seat in the middle of the room and sat down to try to relax.

As she sat there feeling very much alone, she thought of another Sunday she had felt awkward walking into a strange church. She smiled as she considered how that day had marked the coming of a significant change in her life. Yes, she might feel uncomfortable and out of place in this big church, but she now had a peace she hadn't known was possible a couple of months ago.

"Thank you, Lord," she whispered quietly.

The service she experienced was nothing to complain about. The music was beautiful and very professionally done. Her heart warmed when she could join in with the congregational singing. The sermon was practical and challenging. It was good to hear a sermon in person instead of on the radio.

When she reached her car after the service was over, she was glad she had been able to go to church again. As she was pulling out of the parking lot, a thought suddenly occurred to her. She couldn't remember anyone speaking directly to her the entire evening. Some had smiled in her direction, but not a soul had welcomed her or asked her name. Katie tried to remember if she had done anything to avoid personal contact, but all she had really done was walk in and walk out. She wasn't sure what she could have done differently. At least she didn't have to worry about anyone showing up at her door or sending a letter that Lucas would see. No one had the least idea who she was or from where she had come. Nevertheless, she kept her eyes open for another church to try on Wednesday evening.

After a light supper at home, Katie brought out her new books. She read the introductions, forwards, and table of contents of each book. As she put the last one down and prayed one last prayer, she decided to begin with the one about living a victorious Christian life.

She took the book to her favorite room, the small den in the basement. As she made her way down the stairs, she smiled at herself. She had a house full of beautiful and elegant rooms, and she chose to go down to the tiny den in the corner of the basement. Yet for some reason she felt safe in this room … cozy … and at home. She cuddled up on the small couch in front of the unlit fireplace. She took a deep breath and just enjoyed this feeling of freedom. It felt good to be alone and not worry that Lucas might come through the door and discover her relaxing, not working.

Opening the chosen book, she found in the pages what truly seemed like a gold mine. One of the radio talks she'd heard the week before referred to the words of the Bible as better than gold, and now as this book explained the meaning of various verses, she could see the truth of that statement. There were a few points she had already discovered, but most of what she read was brand new.

She had already realized that this "Christianity" business wasn't about religion or a certain church or a system of do's and don'ts. The first sermon on Cornelius had taught her that. She knew from experience that the most important thing was to personally know God through Jesus Christ and what He did on the cross. Sometimes she could close her eyes and almost believe Jesus was seated next to her or at the foot of her bed. Maybe her desperate need for friendship these last lonely months was why she had come to appreciate the "friendship" of Jesus so much.

Yet one fact continuously troubled her. No matter how hard she tried not to, she just kept doing things she knew God didn't want her to do or not doing things she knew she should be doing. She tried to ease her conscience by thinking about how frustrating Lucas could be, but she really knew that didn't excuse her. Many times her circumstances drove her to the brink of despair.

This little book pointed her to places in God's Word that explained why she was having such a hard time. She was trying to do things on her own … trying to be perfect in her own strength. She realized that the old Katie was still there and couldn't manage to be good all the time now, any more than before Jesus saved her. The secret of success seemed to start with giving up and admitting she couldn't do it. Then she must let Jesus live His life through her. She didn't need more patience. Jesus was supposed to be her patience. She didn't need more faith. Jesus was supposed to be her faith. She didn't have to somehow conjure up the strength to be what she knew God wanted her to be or to do what God wanted her to do. She had to surrender all to Him. Evidently once God had control, then she could choose to do right, and He would enable her to do it in His strength.

It all seemed impossible, but the author used so many verses from the Bible, like the ones in Galatians 2, that said she had died when Jesus was crucified. Now she was alive again, and it really wasn't she, but Christ living in her.

She didn't have any idea how long she'd been engrossed in her study until she glanced up at the basement window only to realize that the sun was casting its first rays across the horizon. She laughed in amazement as she realized she'd been reading all night. Katie reluctantly marked her page and mounted the stairs for her bedroom. She mentally noted that she must remember to record these newfound truths in her prayer journal. They were so exciting to her she wanted to share them with someone, and at this point God seemed to be the only one who listened to her.

After only a few hours of sleep, she woke up and forced herself to leave her comfy bed. She knew if she slept too long, she'd never be able to fall asleep at night and besides she didn't want to waste her "vacation" by sleeping too much.

A light breakfast prepared her to race through the basic chores she had planned to complete that day. By the time she was hungry for lunch, she felt satisfied that she could take the rest of the day to do as she pleased.

With a sack lunch in one hand and her book and Bible in the other hand, Katie set off to explore the beautiful woods and meadows that surrounded Lucas' house. She truly didn't feel like this was home, but she was thrilled with the chance to enjoy it all for these next two weeks.

She headed in the direction of the picturesque little bridge that crossed a small meandering stream. The afternoon was actually cloudy and dismal. The sun that had signaled her this morning was now hidden by dark clouds, but Katie didn't care. She felt like roaming and nothing could stop her. Just past the bridge she noticed a path apparently made by the local wildlife disappearing into the woods. Katie quietly entered the shadows made darker by the overcast day. She followed the path taking in all the sights and sounds. She dodged low branches, thorn bushes, and poison ivy as she slowly made her way down the trail. Occasionally she came to a fork and had to decide in which direction to continue, each time hoping she could find her way back.

Once she stopped to watch two playful squirrels, cavorting in a tree. A little further along she saw a snake disappear into the undergrowth beside the pathway. She took her next steps carefully, hoping the small serpent's family wasn't nearby ready to startle her. Up ahead she could see that the path led out into a small meadow surrounded by woods. Just as Katie was about to step out into the open, she spotted a doe and two fawns grazing at the edge of the field. She stood motionless watching the little family eat. Growing weary of standing still, Katie tried to sit down noiselessly, but Mama deer must have detected her presence and her entertainment vanished into the trees.

Once the distraction was gone, Katie noticed she was hungry. Seated on a fallen log, she opened her lunch and her book and read as she ate her food. Long after she'd eaten her last bite she continued her deep reverie in the world of what her life could be and should be in Christ.

In this state she didn't notice the chill in the air as the temperature fell and the wind picked up. Neither did she note how menacing the sky had become or how fierce the approaching clouds appeared. The first thing she did notice was a large droplet of rain landing on her book near the very words she was reading. Three more followed in close succession. She looked up to see dark angry clouds moving in her direction. She stashed her book and Bible in the plastic bag she had brought her lunch in, to protect them from the rain that was increasing by the moment.

As she made her way back through the woods toward home, the trees protected her from much of the rain, but they also made the way much darker. Gradually the wind picked up, whipping the branches above her back and forth, letting more water reach the ground. As the storm grew worse, she tried to hurry but now she was having trouble figuring out which trail to take or even in which direction the house was located. Everything looked different in the rain. The sky above, when she got a glimpse of it through the treetops, was almost as dark as night. The rain came down in torrents now, making it hard to see clearly. She found herself slapped by branches and tripping over hidden roots.

Katie continued stumbling along with a growing fear that she was headed in the wrong direction. Nothing looked really familiar, but she had no choice but to proceed hoping she would come out of the trees. Once she thought she had come to the edge of the woods, but was disappointed to find herself in a small clearing. She stood there briefly, watching the lightning illuminate the sky. Cold, soaking wet, and confused, Katie paused as a new factor added to her uneasiness. Marble-sized hail started to pelt the ground around her and to sting her face and bare arms.

Growing up in Indiana, she had always heard that hail often accompanied a tornado. A gnawing fear began to infiltrate her being. Moved by fear, Katie tried desperately to find something that looked familiar, but to no avail. She tried to quicken her steps only to trip over a root and land in the thorny clutches of a blackberry bush. Katie winced in pain as she carefully extricated herself from its thorny branches and collapsed in frustration at the foot of a large oak tree.

Crumpled up against a fallen log, she cried out to God. "Lord, help me! I can't do it myself. I've done my best, but I just can't figure out the way home. Won't you please help? Please, just point me in the right direction," she pleaded, her tears mixing with the rain.

At just that moment she noticed what she was sitting against. The decaying log had a large limb branching out from each side, making it resemble an arrow. She had spotted this very log soon after she had begun her trek in the woods because it seemed to point directly at the house. Relief permeated her mind. She was sure she was nearly out of the woods and close to shelter.

"Thanks, Lord. You're amazing," she whispered as she limped down the path that would lead her home. That first glimpse of the large house brought such comfort. Katie noticed that for the first time since she had come to live in Lucas' house, it felt like she was going home. If only there were someone waiting there to welcome her … to listen to her harrowing adventure in the storm. Lucas crossed her mind briefly, but she honestly would rather come home to an empty house than to have her new husband there to greet her. She couldn't imagine him giving her any consolation.

Katie breathed another prayer of thanks as she entered the back door. Shivering, she went to adjust the air conditioner. Lucas would disapprove, but he wasn't home and she was cold and tired. Her swollen ankle throbbed as she headed upstairs for a hot bath and dry clothes.

With the bathtub filling she began to shed her wet clothes, but the shrill ring of the telephone interrupted her. Though she was tempted to just let the answering machine take the call, she decided to pick it up.

"Hello," she answered timidly.

"Hello, Katlyn," the familiar voice responded. "How is everything at home? Wayne just talked to his kids back home and they said there was a tornado warning and a touchdown reported not too far from where you are. Is it storming there now?"

"Oh, yes!" Katie couldn't help smiling. "We've got quite a storm going on right now."

"Where are you?" the question came.

"What do you mean, where am I? I'm in the house, of course."

"No, silly," Lucas answered disgustedly. "What room are you in?"

"My bedroom," she replied, wondering why he asked.

"Well, go down to the den in the basement. That's probably the safest place to be in case a tornado comes your way," Lucas answered firmly.

"But I was just about to take a hot bath," Katie protested.

"A hot bath in the middle of a late afternoon storm? What are you thinking, woman? Use your head. You go downstairs immediately and call me when the storm is over. Get a pen and write down this number."

Katie obediently wrote down the number, turned off the bath water, grabbed some dry clothes and a blanket and limped down two flights of stairs, cold and miserable. She had mixed emotions about her husband's demands. He must care a little about her to be so concerned about her safety, but it really felt like he just enjoyed being the boss and ordering her around.

Once downstairs she turned the television on to a local channel to catch any severe weather reports. As she changed into dry clothes she listened, noting that from the look of the weather map, the worst of the storm would soon be beyond the area.

Still feeling chilled to the bone, she wrapped up in a blanket while she combed out her wet tangled hair. When the TV went back to its regular programming, she considered calling Lucas as he had asked; but there was still some lightning and thunder so she decided to wait until she was sure the storm was over. Finally starting to get warm, she snuggled up on the overstuffed couch and soon drifted off to sleep. The piercing ring of the telephone disturbed her slumber and she hopped up disoriented and not sure where the phone was. The only light in the now dark room came from the television, but with its dim illumination she found the phone and picked it up.

Still groggy she was unprepared for her husband's outburst.

"What's the problem there that kept you from calling me back as I asked. Are you going to tell me it's still storming over there? Or did you maybe just forget my simple request that you call? Maybe it just wasn't that important to you to do what your husband asked. Well, I've tried to be patient with you, but it has been three hours and I was beginning to think the whole house blew away. So what's your excuse? Why haven't you called?"

Lucas finally paused giving Katie time to respond. "I fell asleep."

"You did what?" he roared back. "You mean with a storm raging and funnel touchdowns in the area, you just went to sleep. Where are your brains, woman? What possessed you to just go to sleep at a time like that?"

"I'm sorry, but I got caught in the storm, so I was tired and wet, so when I started to warm up, I must have fallen asleep. The telephone woke me up. I'm sorry. I didn't intend to worry you."

"Well, you sure did. I thought of all sorts of things that could have happened. And by the way, how could you have gotten caught in the storm."

"I was taking a walk back in the woods when it started, then I got turned around and had trouble finding the way back. Everything is fine here now. I'm sorry you had to worry. Are you having a good time in Hawaii?" Katie tried to change the subject.

"Oh, as good as could be expected under the circumstances," Lucas growled. "You know how it is. These business slash pleasure trips are never all that you expect them to be."

Lucas hoped as he said these words Katie wouldn't ask for details. He couldn't put how he felt into words. The truth, that Lucas would never admit even to himself, was that he had grown accustomed to having Katie around and he missed her terribly. Most of the others there from his company had their mates with them and seemed to be having a great time. Lucas ended up spending most of his time with an older man named Jerry who had never been married. And after having spent so much time with him, Lucas was beginning to think that his bachelorhood was for the best. He was sure no woman could live with Jerry. It was only the first full day of this "dream vacation" and Lucas already regretted not bringing his wife.

As these thoughts quickly ran through his head, his tone softened. "So how are things going for you? Are you bored to death?"

"No, not really," Katie replied carefully. She dare not let her husband know how much she was enjoying his absence. "I've been doing a lot of reading."

"Really, I never knew you liked to read. What are you reading anyway?" Lucas was curious now.

Not sure how Lucas would respond if he knew all her books were Christian, she answered evasively, "Quite a variety, really. Some friends gave me some books as going away gifts. I just haven't had much opportunity to read until now."

"What do you mean by that?" Lucas spoke up defensively. "I'm not that much a slave driver! You could have read them before."

As usual the conversation had soured. Thinking Katie was trying to subtly make a point, his ego retaliated with the thought, "She's probably reading a bunch of lurid romance novels. Oh well, what did I expect when I married a perfect stranger?"

Katie only smiled unaware of his most recent thoughts. She sensed that his ego was bruised, but was still glad to have his verbal permission to read once he was back.

The conversation seemed abruptly over and they said their mutual goodbyes. Glad to have the phone call over with, Katie fixed a quick supper. Then after her postponed bath she settled down once again to read. It seemed like days ago since she sat in the meadow reading, rather than hours ago. She pondered the truths she was learning, comparing them with the way she had handled today's difficulties. She felt ashamed as she realized that even though she was in the very midst of learning that in her own strength she could do nothing, when trouble came she had immediately attempted to escape her difficulties with her own ingenuity. She wondered if her experience in the woods would have been different had she trusted God and asked for His wisdom from the beginning. But old habits can be hard to overcome. Since her parents' death, she had often been forced to depend on her own resources. How could she ever remember to go to God first? Maybe that was something that would take God's strength, too. She knew that somehow she was going to have to develop the habit of remembering that she had died with Christ and now her new life had to be Christ living out His life through her. It was all so new and refreshing. Now if she could just put these principles to work in real life situations.

CHAPTER 16

The next few days were gloriously free for Katie. She finished whatever work she had planned for each day early in the morning. The rest of these days were spent hiking, reading, and driving. She took long drives each day to familiarize herself with her neighborhood and how to get to stores and businesses. One afternoon she lost track of how long she had been driving and ended up too close to Chicago during rush hour. The multiple lanes and kamikaze drivers darting in and out of traffic terrified her. This adventure taught her a valuable lesson: never let that happen again!

Several times she wasn't sure she would ever find her way home, but she had lots of practice asking God for wisdom. She wondered at times if she was being stupid to drive all over the countryside for no good reason, yet she was afraid that these two weeks would be her only chance to learn her surroundings. There had been little chance to be out since she had come to this area.

By Wednesday she had found a much smaller church about five miles from her home. It wasn't on a main road, so her traveling had paid off in this way at least. As she entered the church for midweek Bible Study and Prayer, she found the group small but warm. It brought tears to her eyes because it reminded her of the precious friends she had made at Patti's church and how much she missed them.

Katie was somewhat alarmed, however, to notice that she was involuntarily putting up a wall between herself and these friendly believers. Maybe it was partly because she couldn't help imagining how Lucas would react if someone from this church ended up knocking on his door. Fearing this very thing, she told all inquirers that she was vacationing in the area. She tried to soothe her conscience about the deception by recalling that Lucas had called these two weeks her vacation, but she still felt uneasy.

Katie was also afraid that part of her problem in mixing with new people was the fact that she had been so separated from other people since coming to live with Lucas. Except for infrequent trips to the store and restaurants and the tennis outing with Dr. Tom and Amy, Katie's sole companion had been her husband, and their relationship was growing more comfortable but certainly not congenial. Yet what could she do about it? It was obvious that Lucas was so afraid someone would discover their unusual arrangement that he sheltered his new wife from the outside world.

Katie didn't like this feeling … this need to withdraw inside herself. This wasn't normal for her at all. The thought came to her that she would never be free to be herself again. She felt depressed and couldn't concentrate on what was being said in the service.

When the pastor mentioned breaking up into small prayer groups, fear enveloped her. The growing apprehension was trying to paralyze her as she moved to sit with one younger and two older women who had encouraged the newcomer to join them. Once on her feet, she was overwhelmed with an abrupt inclination to bolt and run out of the church.

Suddenly words she had read recently came to her mind. "Apart from me you can do nothing," and "I can do everything through him who gives me strength." In a matter of moments she chose to believe those words and sent out a call for help to her Friend and God.

The ladies in her group accepted her shyness without question and assured her she was welcome to pray aloud or pray silently whatever she chose to do. As she sat quietly listening to the prayers of the other ladies she felt herself relax. Praying silently, she experienced a calm assurance that she could trust God with her life even though sometimes she felt like she was tangled in a giant web.

After her work was done on Thursday, Katie spent an hour reading and finished her first "vacation" book. She had thoroughly enjoyed it, yet she still felt so inadequate to put all she had learned into practice. Though tempted to turn to page one and go through the same book again, Katie looked over the remaining books once again to decide.

As she picked up the book on marriage she smiled sadly. On the cover were the words, "For Every Married Couple."

"I bet the author never ran into a marriage like ours," Katie mumbled out loud. Tears came to her eyes as she considered whether or not to even read this book at all. Surely there was nothing in its pages that she could apply to her situation. For just a moment she let herself remember the dreams she had as a teenager about what life would be like once she found her Prince Charming. She seldom let her mind drift in that direction because it never failed to depress her. Yet this time, armed with her new found knowledge of the previous book, she resisted the temptation to dwell on her circumstances. She made a conscious choice to believe that God was in control. Taking a deep breath, Katie carried the book on marriage down the stairs.

"I'd better read this one while Lucas is gone," she thought. "No telling how he would react if he caught me reading a book on marriage."

Before she could do any more reading though, she determined to take a shopping trip. The one thing her husband had asked her to do while he was gone was to buy a new outfit. A week after his return from Hawaii they were scheduled to go with the "big boss" Mr. Barnes and his wife to dinner and a baseball game. She really had no idea what the proper attire for a professional baseball game was, but she was beginning to understand her husband's preferences. He like casual but feminine, so that was what she was seeking.

The young bride could also detect that her husband was very nervous about the coming get together. He seemed to feel like his promotion depended solely on how this evening went. And Katie sensed that Lucas wasn't sure she was ready for the event. He had commented that he would coach her on how he wanted her to behave when he returned from his trip. Of course, his lack of confidence had stung her, but she had continued to put a wall up to protect herself from the totally inconsiderate remarks that came her way regularly.

Nevertheless, she had decided to do her very best to be what Lucas wanted for this occasion. If he didn't get this promotion, she didn't want to be the one blamed.

After several hours of shopping, she chose an outfit that she thought would make the best impression on all concerned. On the way home she stopped for an early supper so she wouldn't have to bother cooking tonight. By the time she approached home it was starting to get dark and she noticed how well you could see a side view of Lucas' beautiful house from the road a couple of hundred feet from their driveway. Any view of the house from the road in front was completely blocked by trees, but with the security floodlights Lucas had installed, there was quite a nice view of their residence at a bend in the road. Since the lights went on automatically at dusk, she always came home to a well-lit house when she was out at night. She was so distracted by the view that she almost missed the fact that a van was leaving her driveway just as she was ready to turn into it. Puzzled at first by the strange vehicle, she soon decided someone had just needed to turn around. Katie couldn't get over an uneasy feeling about the incident, but she chided herself for being a sissy and pushed aside her uneasiness.

Dressed for bed she tucked the new book under her arm and with a blueberry muffin in one hand and a glass of milk in the other, she made her way down to her favorite room in the basement. She wasn't full of anticipation as she had been with the other book, but dutifully opened it and turned to the first page. The sooner she finished this volume the sooner she could start on the next.

Yet in spite of her negative attitude, she was soon reading with more interest than she had expected. The author spoke with such authority about improving good marriages, repairing broken ones, and even bringing life to relationships that had been loveless from the beginning. Maximizing love in the marriage relationship was presented as such a necessity and also such a possibility that she found herself feeling almost hopeful. This feeling alone immediately stirred fear in her … fear of failure … fear of being hurt. Up to this moment her loveless marriage had not significantly hurt her emotionally because she had forced herself not to contemplate success. You were never disappointed if you never let yourself expect anything. True, she had considered the possibility that love could develop between Lucas and herself and had even been depressed when that seemed more and more unlikely, but she had never really let her emotions get involved. Frankly, she wasn't even sure she liked Lucas.

As she turned each page, she felt herself being challenged to make some significant changes. Until now she had thought she had done well to stay even tempered and non-retaliatory when her husband revealed his frequent impatience or sometimes just his icy demeanor, but suddenly she was questioning whether or not that was enough.

She felt a battle within as she argued with the author. Given her unusual circumstances surely no one would ask or expect anything more from her … not even God. She certainly received nothing in return. Every attempt to warm up to her husband had been met with immediate coldness. How could God expect her to give love without receiving any? Wasn't marriage supposed to be this fifty-fifty proposition of give and take?

The more she read, the more she saw her answer plainly. God's Word clearly taught she was to love her mate, not because he deserved it, not because she was "in love" with him, but just because God said to do it. The truth wasn't as obvious for wives as for husbands with the glaring statement, "Husbands, love your wives," but it was still there. You could see it in the verses where Paul told the older women to teach the younger women to "love their husbands." How strange to think of this as something she needed to learn … to work at.

Then something within fought back with thoughts that her situation was not normal. How many women married a stranger for a sum of money? How many men married a woman so he could get a promotion? But as if sparring in a boxing match, other thoughts jumped up to be considered. What about women in other times and places who had their marriages arranged by their families? Sometimes they had not even seen their spouse until the wedding day. Surely this happened in the days these Bible verses were first composed. Perhaps this is why they had to be taught to love. Could it be that God expected that from her? But she had no one to teach her. How could she possibly learn to love a man who had no love for her?

Back and forth her mind went, first accusing then excusing her. Finally the idea came to her that perhaps this very book was sent by God to be her teacher. That thought calmed her spirit.

With her mind and heart weary from the battle, Katie set the book aside and knelt beside the couch. "Lord," she began. "I confess I'm afraid to love Lucas. I can't imagine his loving me back, and I don't want to feel the pain of loving someone who doesn't return that love. But I've heard Your voice today and You say I have to learn to love my husband. Well, there's simply no way I can do that unless You do it through me. In that last book I learned that Your strength is made perfect in my weakness, so I guess I'm in good shape. I've never felt less adequate for any task in my life.

"So, Lord, here I am. I confess to You I can't do this on my own. I guess I'm saying that I'm willing, but You're going to have to do this through me. Help me to deal with the fear of failure and the pain of rejection because I'm sure both are bound to come. I'm in Your hands. Help me to do what is right."

As Katie moved from the floor back to the couch, she picked the book up with renewed commitment. No matter what kind of husband Lucas was, she was going to become the wife God wanted her to be. As she immersed herself in her study, she was at once both intrigued and almost overwhelmed. The whole concept of her marriage growing into a living, loving relationship exhilarated her, but the putting into practice was so new to her. There was too much to consider. Where should she begin?

She ran up to the office to find some paper to begin taking notes. One chapter listed four steps to a better marriage. The first was to speak well about your mate and to your mate ...doing good things for him, not out of duty but as a gift. Then the instructions took a step further by suggesting you build up your husband partly by praising him, but even more by responding to him with respect and admiration. Included was a decision to never be critical of your partner in word, deed, or even thought.

Next came sharing ... your life ... your emotions. That sounded so simplistic, yet Katie had been very careful to do the opposite. She had shielded herself instead of sharing herself. Could she ever do otherwise?

The fourth step, believe it or not, was by touching ... not in a sexual way, but in a very caring way. This, too, Katie recognized would be easier said than done. Though she and Lucas had spent many nights together, Katie had never once reached out and touched her husband's face or arm in the light of day. Would that kind of familiarity be welcomed, or would Lucas respond with icy surprise?

Katie decided that to make this change in behavior she would have to determine to take specific actions toward her husband. She would have to consciously choose to change her attitude as well. She found herself wishing she had a picture of Lucas to prepare herself mentally for these changes, but pictures were one thing that was noticeably missing in this grand house that appeared to have everything. On that first day's inventory of the property she had hoped to find a photo album or framed picture that would satisfy her curiosity about what the first wife had looked like. Yet not one single snapshot could be found.

As she pondered this, she suddenly had an idea — the attic. She had seen an opening in the ceiling of the library and assumed there was some sort of attic or storage up there, but she had never investigated. This would be her perfect opportunity. She felt her excitement build as she scurried up the stairs feeling like a mischievous child looking for hidden Christmas gifts.

The hinged covering in the ceiling easily opened to reveal a retractable ladder. The switch for the lights was on the wall close to the attic's opening. As she flipped on the switch, she gazed in wonder at what felt like another world above her home. The room itself was large with unfinished walls and a low unfinished ceiling. The area looked as if it had once been organized in an orderly fashion then later ransacked — or maybe additional storage was added carelessly. Boxes were overturned with contents half spilled out on the floor.

Suitcases and storage chests were thrown in a corner, not stacked, but all in a heap.

The feeling that she was intruding into someone's personal business was so strong she almost left without looking further, yet she decided this was her house, and Lucas had never forbidden her to come up here, so she began to explore. The suitcases and trunks contained women's clothing, no doubt Adrian's. Apparently it was easier for Lucas to just get them out of sight rather than deal with finding a place to dispose of them. Katie could tell that Adrian only wore the very best designer apparel, even though the clothes were thrown together without any order.

How Katie wished she could find some pictures. Not only did she want a picture of her husband, but she felt a need to see what Adrian looked like. Was it just curiosity or a real desire to understand Lucas better? Whatever the reason, Katie moved from box to box, examining the contents. It wasn't long until she realized that all the thrown together boxes belonged to Adrian. Looking around at the mess, Katie could only imagine what a tremendous emotional experience for her husband Adrian's death had been. She couldn't really imagine her aloof husband with that much visible emotion. Losing Adrian must have really changed him.

Then she saw something behind a large bag full of shoes. It was a beautifully carved wooden box about two feet long, one foot wide and maybe a foot tall. The box had been broken and was lying on its side with the contents spread across the floor. Katie stooped down and, trembling slightly, picked up an album full of pictures. Opening to the first page she was face to face with the handsome image of the man who was her husband. At his side in each picture was a dramatically beautiful woman. Her hair was full and dark, falling in soft waves around her shoulders. As she turned each page of the wedding album, she was struck by the beauty and intensity of this woman's eyes.

Turning her attention to the bridegroom's face, she realized that she had never met this handsome young man who looked incredibly happy. She had to admit they looked like the perfect couple. The last page showed a picture of her husband and the other woman arm in arm, waving, joyful, obviously leaving for a no doubt storybook honeymoon. Katie was surprised to feel a new emotion creeping over her. She recognized that she was actually jealous of Lucas' first wife.

Later downstairs while viewing a video of Lucas and Adrian's honeymoon, the feeling was joined by anxiety. The video presented a very graceful, self-assured woman. Katie simply could find no fault in her. No wonder Lucas was so cool toward Katie. She felt so inadequate. How could she ever hope to find a place in the heart of a man who was married to the perfect woman? It was obvious in this video that he adored her. She could barely imagine that this carefree young man was the same man to whom she was married.

When the video was over, Katie felt despair threaten to overtake her. A few hours before she had been so hopeful. She could almost imagine her relationship with Lucas evolving into something warm and wonderful. Now a nagging voice seemed to scoff at the very idea. How could she even imagine such a miracle after seeing the goddess that was stolen from him by her untimely death.

Yet before Katie was totally engulfed in self-pity and discouragement, she turned her thoughts to God and remembered a verse she had been memorizing. It was Matthew 19:26, and Jesus had said the words, "With man this is impossible, but with God all things are possible."

She sat for several minutes just feeling the warmth of those words. She smiled through her tears as she spoke to God. "Ok, Lord, as impossible as all this seems, I'm right now making a decision to believe You. Surely it must be right for me to love my husband and my husband to love me.

Well, I'm willing to do whatever it takes if You'll help me. Show me what You want me to do, and I'll expect a miracle from You. Thanks for always being there for me."

Suddenly realizing she had been up half the night, Katie returned the video and pictures to the attic. That is, all except for one picture of her husband standing in front of a quaint looking cottage. This picture she tucked safely into her journal. She would use this to help her visualize her plan to show Lucas the love that God commanded her to have for her husband.

CHAPTER 17

Friday and Saturday were spent relaxing and practicing a new attitude toward Lucas Michael Lehman. It was a constant battle at first to discipline herself to think only positive thoughts about him. Was it wrong to be glad she still had another week of "vacation" before he came home? She wondered when he would call next and if she could begin to show a difference on the telephone.

On Sunday she went back to the smaller church she had attended on Wednesday. This time she anticipated the problems she might have being around strangers, and she asked God specifically for help to be herself among these "brothers and sisters" in Christ. A radio preacher had described those who had trusted Christ as their Savior as brothers and sisters. He had spoken of the "family" of God. She felt as if she needed family right now.

As she drove home Sunday evening after the service, Katie pondered the fact that after Wednesday night prayer meeting she had no idea when she would see these Christian people again. Her husband would be home again next Sunday, which meant she would not be going back to church. Her concentration was so intense she almost missed her driveway. The thought occurred to her that it was strange that she hadn't noticed the break in the trees where she could see the house illuminated by the security floodlights. As she approached the final bend in the long drive, she realized that the security lights were not on. She immediately took her foot from the accelerator, her mind racing to ascertain the situation. Her headlights now faintly illuminated a large van parked in front of the garage. When she saw a figure coming from the house carrying something, she put her car in reverse and backed out. Her heart pounded as an apprehensive feeling permeated her. Katie pulled into a drive across the street, out of view of the intruders, and turned off the headlights.

What should she do? Suddenly she remembered the cell phone Lucas kept in the glove compartment. She retrieved the phone and dialed 911. Quickly she gave her name and address and reported her observations, commenting that she feared someone was burglarizing her home at that moment. The voice on the telephone cautioned her to stay where she was and a unit would be sent immediately.

Just then Katie noticed the van at the end of her driveway. She could barely see it because the headlights had not been turned on. The van moved out into the road, only turning on the headlights as it passed in front of her. Without hesitation she tossed the phone into the seat and started her car, pulling out behind them. All she could think about was that some crook was getting away with Lucas' nice things, and she couldn't let them do that. She at least had to get the license plate number of that van.

She realized right away that it would be hard to get the number inconspicuously because the van was speeding noticeably, and she would have to get pretty close to be able to read the plate. She tried to match their speed without closing the gap between the vehicles too quickly, but suddenly the van turned down a side road. Once out of sight she floored the gas pedal to make up the distance. As she turned onto the new road, she saw that her efforts had succeeded in getting her much closer so she'd better catch up now. With that decision made, she once again accelerated, closing the distance quickly, that is until the van ahead increased its speed as well. When the van had to slow to make another turn, Katie had her chance. She came up on their bumper just in time to read the numbers. Then she continued straight down the road while the van turned to the right. A short distance down the road, Katie pulled over to the side of the road to write down the number before she forgot it. She noticed headlights in her rearview mirror but didn't look up from her writing until the vehicle passed by. To her horror she saw a van that looked exactly like the one she had been chasing. Were the thieves on to her? Had they guessed what she was doing? What should she do? She watched as the van slowed to a stop some distance ahead of her.

"Lord, help me know what to do!" she whispered.

Just then she noticed a house up the road and on the left with all the lights on inside and outside of the house. There were eight or ten cars parked in the drive, and she could see some kids in the yard, jumping on a trampoline.

She put her car in gear and headed for the party. Hopefully there was safety in numbers. As she pulled into the driveway, she could see that the van ahead had turned around and was coming her way. She turned off the engine and ducked down in the seat so she couldn't be seen from behind. She hoped the occupants of the van would think she had left her car and joined the group in the yard.

As she crouched in the front seat, she heard a vehicle pull onto the gravel behind her. For what seemed an eternity there was no sound except for the guests at the party. Finally the vehicle backed out and slowly pulled away from the scene.

She waited a little longer then sat up just in time to see a couple of teenaged boys approaching her car. They seemed friendly enough so she cautiously opened her window a couple of inches. Before they had a chance to question her, she blurted out, "Could you tell me in which direction Walker Street is?"

When the boys pointed in the direction the van had just taken and gave further instructions, she thanked them and backed to the end of the driveway. She waved and smiled sheepishly at the boys still watching her, then she backed out and took off in the opposite direction away from Walker Street.

"Oh well," she thought. "They'll just think I'm an incompetent female."

Two police cars with all lights flashing were parked outside her home when she arrived. She suddenly felt shy and awkward, almost as if she had done something wrong. An officer approached her as she opened her door.

"Are you Katlyn Montgomery?" he asked seriously.

"Yes," she answered simply.

"And do you reside here with Lucas Lehman?" came the next question.

"Yes," she answered suddenly bewildered. "That is, Lucas is my husband. I guess I accidentally gave my maiden name. We haven't been married long, and I guess I was nervous when I called 911. Oh dear, I guess I hung up on them when I got distracted because I saw the van pull out, and I was afraid they'd get away so I followed them, and I guess I forgot about the phone call," Katie rambled on nervously.

"Why don't we go inside, Mrs. Lehman?" the officer said politely. "I can ask you some more questions in there, if that's all right with you?"

"Sure, sir, but before we lose any more time, I have the license plate number of the dark blue late model van that pulled out of here. Shouldn't you call it in or something so someone can be looking for it?" Katie offered awkwardly.

The sheriff went to his car and relayed the information on his radio then accompanied Katie into the house and began questioning her about all the details of the evening and exactly what items were missing. She walked through the house making mental notes of what was missing — computer equipment, VCR, two DVD players, three television sets, including the one with the huge screen, a few pieces of furniture, and jewelry from Lucas' room.

She couldn't help chuckling as she entered her own room. It was obvious from the mess that the thieves had expected to find some jewelry in her room, but other than the wedding band she was wearing she had no expensive jewelry. The jewelry she did own was spilled on the floor. "Bet that was a big disappointment," she said under her breath.

The ring of the telephone interrupted her thoughts. She looked toward the officer at her side. He nodded slightly so she picked up the phone. Her husband's voice greeted her.

"Hello, Katlyn. How is everything going at home?"

"I guess I'd have to say not that well right now. There's been a robbery," Katie responded weakly, wishing there was some better way to break the news.

At first Lucas went into a tirade of questions, one after another, without pausing for answers. When he finally slowed down, Katie began to speak.

"Someone in a van burglarized your house this evening while I was out, but we have their license plate number, so I'm hoping the police can find them right away and then you can get all your nice things back, maybe even before you get home next week."

Lucas interrupted. "I thought you said they broke in while you were out. How did the police get the plate number?"

"Well, actually they were still here when I drove in, so I backed out and parked across the street until they left, and then I followed them until I could read the license number," the young wife replied innocently.

"You did what?!!" the voice on the other end exploded. "Are you crazy, woman? What were you thinking? I guess it's just not safe to leave you at home alone. Of all the stupid, idiotic things to do. You could have been attacked, even killed and for what? Then where would I be? Didn't you think about what could happen?

Lucas ceased the attack as quickly as he had begun. After a brief silence Katie replied softly in spite of the lump in her throat. "No, I guess I didn't."

Lucas winced as he read from her tone that he had wounded her. He hadn't meant to do that. It was just that in one moment it had flashed through his mind what his life would go back to if his mate were no longer there, and it terrified him.

"Are the police still there?" he asked abruptly.

"Yes, they are."

"Let me talk to one of them."

Once the phone was in the hands of the officer, she walked across the room, not really wanting to overhear the conversation. She felt tired and depressed. She had tried to do what seemed best at the moment, but now she felt stupid for not thinking about the danger her instincts had lured her into. She just wanted all the people to leave so she could go to bed and forget about everything that had happened.

Soon the officer handed the phone back to her.

"Katlyn, I'm calling Dr. Tom. He and Amy had to come home early. You can stay with them until I get back. I'll take the first flight I can get home."

"Oh, no," Katie blurted out. "That's really not necessary. I'll be fine, and you don't have to cut your trip short."

"No, Katlyn, I've made my decision. The policeman said a window was broken in the sunroom. That's how they got in, so you can't possibly stay there until it's fixed. And I don't want you there alone right now anyway, at least until they catch the criminals. I'll call Tom and Amy right now, so get together a few things to take with you. I'm not sure how soon I can get a flight out of here."

"But, Lucas," Katie interrupted.

"No discussion. I'll see you soon, Katlyn."

Then all she heard was the dial tone.

CHAPTER 18

Dr. Tom and Amy tried desperately to entertain Katie and comfort her after her ordeal, but all she really wanted was to be alone. She told herself that socializing with other human beings was a rarity in her life these days, and she should be happy for the opportunity, yet she had so little in common with the sophisticated Amy that she had trouble carrying on a conversation. Maybe that was why Katie actually found herself counting the hours until her husband's return.

When she first realized he was really cutting short his paradise vacation, she felt a pang of regret surge through her. That meant her "vacation" was cut short also, and she would miss her opportunity to attend church again. She wondered how long it would be before she would be able to go to church.

As Monday's hours crept slowly by, she changed her attitude, and tried to remember all the plans she had made to show love to her husband. His flight was due to arrive early Tuesday morning. Though eager to get back home, she was growing more nervous about her new role as "loving" wife. She tried to resign herself to the fact that her early efforts would probably be rejected, but hopefully, in time, things would change. She really couldn't help entertaining the hope that somehow Lucas would respond soon and return some love her way.

Katie would have been shocked had she realized all the emotions coursing through her stolid looking husband on the long ride back to the Midwest. His days away from Katie had forced him to admit that he missed her presence. The idea that she could have suddenly been removed from his life had truly jolted him. His mind went into a self defense mode, going over "logical" reasons that he would not want to lose Katie. He was doing anything he could to keep from admitting his emotions were involved. He scolded himself for being weak and determined anew that he would not again fall prey to a woman's designs. He could surely *appreciate* this woman without all the emotional baggage.

Yet all his structured determination threatened to melt the moment his eyes found her pretty face waiting beside Dr. Tom at the airport. Her shy smile and searching eyes demanded a response. He told himself that he had to play the part of the returning beloved for the sake of Dr. Tom who was watching, but it felt oh so good to hold Katie close then gently kiss her forehead.

A new question emerged during their brief embrace. Lucas thought he detected a definite positive response. Was she too playing the "happy newlywed" role? Or had the old adage "absence makes the heart grow fonder" been true for his young wife? In the long run this could prove to be a problem, but right now he would enjoy the moment.

With little conversation Dr. Tom went for the car, leaving the couple to retrieve Lucas' luggage. Once alone, Lucas asked quietly, "Are you all right?"

The timid smile that accompanied her words warmed him. "I'm fine, but I'm glad you're here."

Katie was surprised as she realized that her answer was true. As she looked directly into the eyes of the man she had made a choice to love, she felt drawn to him for the very first time since their marriage.

"Thank you, Lord," she prayed silently. "Only now do I really see that it's possible for me to love Lucas. Please make it so."

That same moment when their eyes met left Lucas slightly shaken. Always before, he could read his young wife's eyes. Why not now? Even more disconcerting was the feeling that Katlyn could see his inward feelings. The discomfort was heightened by the fact that he couldn't even understand himself. He made an attempt to put up his guard, but the warmth of her look didn't disappear, and after all he did have to put on a good show in front of Tom. He would worry about all this later.

The conversation on the way home was rather disjointed. One moment they would be discussing the trip to Hawaii, and the next moment one of the men would ask for some detail about the burglary. Both Katie and Lucas were glad when Dr. Tom dropped them off at their house, and they were finally alone.

At first Lucas had to see that the repairman he had contacted while still in Hawaii had fixed the window sufficiently. After that as they were surveying the house noting what had been stolen, the phone rang. Katie was relieved when Lucas reported that the van had been located, and the stolen items retrieved. She had felt responsible for the loss of her husband's valuables even though she could think of nothing she could have done to prevent it.

They were down in the little den in the basement when the call came. Though Lucas hadn't been all that troubled about his losses, the news still brought some closure to the situation. Lucas sat down on Katie's favorite couch with a contented sigh.

"By the way, the officer on the phone said the license plate number aided their search." Lucas stated unenthusiastically, "But I still say if anything like that ever happens in the future, you stay put and let the police do the chasing."

"I'm sure you're right," Katie answered simply. "Honestly, I was reacting, not really thinking."

As she talked, Katie sat down on the couch beside her husband. The action seemed simple enough, but for both parties the significance was great. On the one hand, Katie was forcing herself to be the wife she wanted to be. Though still uncomfortable in this man's presence, she willed herself not to act that way. If she was going to love this man, she must choose to do so and then act as if she truly loved him.

Lucas, too, was not comfortable, but for different reasons. He was waging a battle with his own emotions. He didn't want to admit how much he had longed to be back with the woman seated next to him. Was he just imagining it or was she somehow different — warmer, more receptive? And if she was, how should he react? As soon as his mind asked the question, he knew the answer. Though all his instincts wanted to draw her close and enjoy this new sensitivity, he must be strong. Whatever conniving she had done while he was away, he was determined that there could be no emotional attachment. Not this time. He would not repeat the past — never again.

So with new resolve, he turned to Katie matter-of-factly and announced, "Well, at least my coming back early will give us more time to get ready for the big outing with the boss and his wife. Remember, that's the basic reason you're here, and this one evening may be the basis for Old Man Barnes' decision about my promotion. We've got to do our homework on this one so you don't blow it for me next week."

The coldness in his voice was calculated to break the spell of the moment. Inwardly, Lucas cringed at his own words. He knew they would hurt Katie. He had to do something to kill that glow he saw in her eyes — the warmth that threatened to melt his own resolve.

The cold, calculated remarks were sufficient for the task. Katie felt as if she had been slapped. Her ego was totally deflated, all confidence gone. Her eyes glistened with moisture, threatening to overflow her eyelids. She silently cried out to her Heavenly Father for help. She tried to sound in control as she responded. "I guess I'm ready whenever you are."

At least she wasn't looking directly in his eyes any more. His matter-of-fact glance caught the moist eyes, yet he didn't feel good about it. He had to reassure himself that Katie's discomfort had been unavoidable.

CHAPTER 19

The next several days were spent going over basic details of their lives. Lucas thought it important they be aware of the elemental particulars of their past: family names, birthdays, favorite things. They also had to come up with an explanation of how they met, etc. Katie was adamant that she wouldn't lie outright, but obviously they couldn't give all the facts. The story they came up with that Katie would agree to was that they were introduced by a mutual acquaintance. Once they realized that each perfectly met the other's needs, they married after a brief courtship. Lucas made it clear that any details given the Barnes had to be believable. He repeatedly reminded Katie how important her performance would be. She must make no mistakes, or the whole marriage farce would be for nothing.

Each night as Katie pondered her day, long after Lucas' breathing became deep and slow, she questioned how she could possibly accomplish her new determination. She tried each day to love the man she lived with, but his constant tutoring emphasized the shallowness of their relationship. She tried to do loving things to prove her affection, yet his cool distance frustrated her and often left her near tears.

By the time the big day came, she was near despair. She had difficulty believing she could ever have a close relationship with this iceberg. Nothing she did made a difference.

She felt she had failed utterly and though she never formulated the words, she subconsciously felt that God had failed, too.

As she dressed for the big event, she had little confidence that they could ever pull it off. Though she honestly wanted to love her husband, she couldn't imagine convincing anyone that she and Lucas were a loving couple.

Lucas was also nervous. He had struggled all week to keep Katie at an arm's length, but the additional warmth in her personality was making her hard to resist. He was feeling the strain of what was at stake, and it left him fidgety and irritable. He knew the boss to be very perceptive at times. Mr. Barnes was the only one at the station that somehow seemed to suspect that Lucas was having marital problems with Adrian. He never understood how, but the old codger had an uncanny way of sensing things. If Mr. Barnes had any idea of the truth about their marriage, Lucas was sure that not only would he lose the promotion, he'd probably lose his job altogether.

Lucas and Katie were to meet the Barnes at the Chicago Cubs stadium, then have a late dinner after the game. The ride to the stadium was quiet except for occasional reminders from Lucas of how Katie should act or what she should say. When they were almost to their seats but still out of earshot, Lucas leaned over and whispered huskily, "If you blow this tonight, I'll never forgive you."

With no time to recover, Katie suddenly felt sick. She was almost dizzy with fear as she heard Lucas introduce her. Though trying her best, she felt stiff and unfriendly. Just when she thought she could take no more, Mrs. Barnes spoke up.

"Katlyn, my dear, could you help me find the ladies' room. I so hate to go alone in these huge stadiums."

Katie agreed, glad for the change, but the warning look Lucas gave her was disconcerting. When they were almost to their destination, Mrs. Barnes ran into an old friend and began a conversation. Katie wanted a private moment to pray, so she excused herself and went ahead. Once alone in the restroom stall, Katie silently cried out to God.

"Lord, I just can't do this. I'm trying my best, but it's not working. The harder I try the worse things get. I just can't do it." That was when she realized her mistake. She'd been doing it all herself again, not really trusting God to live His life through her. Now in humility she quietly gave up. "Lord, please do it through me. I ask that you somehow let me be myself. Live through me and help me be the loving wife I so desperately want to be. At least tonight Lucas can't openly rebuff my love. I need Your help. Truly I can't do it myself."

Oh, what peace sparked deep within her! Suddenly she felt almost an anticipation for the coming evening. Surely this challenge was included in the verse, "I can do everything through him who gives me strength."

When Mrs. Barnes stepped in the door, she looked pleased. "Oh, my dear Katlyn, you look so much better. I was a little afraid you were feeling ill."

"To be perfectly honest I wasn't feeling very well, but I'm doing much better now."

Lucas was desperately struggling to focus on Mr. Barnes' discussion of the condition of the Cubs players. His mind was in turmoil, thinking about the floundering he and Katie had done in the first minutes of this important evening. As he glanced up nervously, his eyes fell on the two women approaching them, chatting easily as if they were close friends. Lucas could only stare speechlessly as Katie seated herself to his right in a relaxed confident manner. The thought came to him that he'd never met this poised young woman before. She was vivacious, yet in control; laughing, yet not giddy; everything he could have hoped for in a model wife.

Katie leaned close and whispered in his ear. "Relax, Luke. I called in reinforcements. Everything is under control."

Then she smiled, winked, and patted his knee.

He felt her touch long after she moved her hand. Suddenly he plunged into the game. All of the things he'd wanted to do these last couple of months, but dared not, he could do now. Katie would realize it was all an act. He was safe to play the part of a loving husband. What a release! And with no strings attached.

Katie's view was a little different. Every attempt she'd made to show her husband her blossoming love for him had been instantly rebuffed. Here was her chance to be the loving wife she truly wanted to be, and if her husband had any sense, he'd have to respond in kind. Even though she realized his part would be only an act, she'd enjoy the moment. So the afternoon and evening were spent exchanging loving looks, playful teasing, and meaningful touches.

Katie continued to refer to her husband as Luke, while he found himself using the pet name Kitten for his mate. He had actually thought of her that way since the first time he'd seen her in her apartment — frightened but not so much that she wouldn't use her claws to defend herself.

Their victory was overwhelming. The Barnes were above all else impressed with the love expressed in the couple's eyes when they exchanged glances. At dinner when questioned, the young couple revealed their first impression of each other. Katie admitted she was intimidated by his good looks and his self confidence. "Luke" honestly revealed that he was immediately enchanted by her quiet beauty that seemed to be as much inward as outward.

When the two couples finally parted, Mrs. Barnes assured Katie they would have to get together again sometime soon. Mr. Barnes congratulated the younger man on his matrimonial choice.

"Well, Lucas," he offered. "I admit I thought you were mistaken in not marrying sooner, but now I can see your lovely wife was worth the wait. I'm sure with that kind of backing at home, you'll go far at the station."

Back in the car alone at last, Katie and Lucas breathed a sigh of relief. Lucas was the first to speak. "We pulled it off, Katlyn. We both deserve an academy award for that performance."

"Performance?" Katie replied briefly, but meaningfully.

"Yeah, performance," he emphasized. "You know what I mean. All that stuff back there. The pretending, the mushy talk, the…well…that…Come on, you *know* what I'm talking about!"

"Yes, dear," Katie replied with a sly smile. "I know *exactly* what you mean."

That statement plunged them into silence, both busy with their own thoughts. Lucas was wondering if he'd gone too far tonight to return to their previous "safe" relationship. Katie was hoping they would never return to the inhibited relationship they'd shared until now. It felt so good just to be herself. She had really enjoyed the presence of the charming thoughtful man with whom she had spent the evening. She hoped and prayed that the charming Lucas would surface again.

CHAPTER 20

The next weeks were a roller coaster existence. The news soon came that Lucas had secured the coveted promotion. Mr. Barnes wasted no time after their evening together in welcoming the younger man into the new position. Yet it didn't take Lucas long to discover that even attaining this dream didn't bring the satisfaction in life for which he had hoped. There was still that gnawing emptiness that nothing in his life seemed capable of filling. Sometimes he felt himself seethe with anger toward Adrian. He blamed his former wife for his present discontent. Surely, if she had never betrayed him, Lucas would be not only successful, but also happy now. Katie tried in varying degrees to continue to show her mate that she had not been pretending. Lucas couldn't deny the growing attraction he felt for the new Katlyn, so he fought a constant battle with his emotions. His attitude would soften in response to her natural warmth; then he would will his character to be aloof and unresponsive. He found himself stooping to making cutting, unkind remarks to accomplish his purpose. When his arrows met their mark, he fought off the remorse he was tempted to feel.

To complicate matters, Katie's health seem to be failing. She assumed the emotional strain was the cause of her increasing bouts with nausea and depression. Even the chaotic events that preceded her marriage had not taken the toll on her emotions that these difficult days seemed to be doing. Somehow she successfully hid her condition from her husband until one Friday morning late in September. She had just put her husband's breakfast on the table in the sunroom when she realized she was going to be sick. Her sudden disappearance piqued his curiosity so he followed her just in time to find her in the bathroom obviously ill. When she came out, slightly pale and shaken, Lucas spoke in a steady unemotional tone. "How long has this been going on?"

"Not long," Katie offered too quickly.

Without another word Lucas disappeared into the den, leaving his wife with that ugly feeling of guilt she had often succumbed to lately. She never quite understood what she was guilty of, but she constantly sensed her husband's displeasure.

After stumbling up the stairs, she fell across her bed and released the flood of tears that had been threatening to escape all morning.

"What's wrong with me?" she wondered. "This just isn't like me. How long she smothered her sobs in her pillow she didn't know, but when she finally turned over she was startled to see her husband watching from the foot of her bed.

"Hurry and change your clothes," he stated firmly. "You have an appointment with Dr. Tom as soon as we can get into his office. He's going to see you before his appointments begin."

"I don't need a doctor," Katie retorted. "I'm sure this will pass soon. It's probably just a touch of the flu."

"Let me know when you're ready to leave," was his only reply as he left the room.

Dr. Tom's office was only a couple of blocks from Lucas' office so he dropped Katlyn off at the curb and promised to be back after he'd taken care of a few things at work. He made the mistake, however, of taking a couple of phone calls while he was there and got back to Dr. Tom's office later than he had expected.

Katie jumped up to meet him when he walked into the waiting room.

"Well, what did Dr. Tom say was wrong with you?" Lucas wanted to know.

"I'll tell you in the car," was all Katie would say.

"I want to talk to Tom before I go," Lucas stated firmly.

"He's with a patient now. Come on, let's go," she urged, taking hold of her husband's arm and almost pulling him out the door.

Once in the car Lucas turned to face his wife. "Ok, we're in the car now. What is wrong with you?"

"Nothing is wrong with me," Katie started in.

"Don't you try to tell me there's nothing wrong with you. Two hours ago you were obviously sick. Now tell me the truth. What did Tom say?" Lucas demanded.

"Oh, Lucas, I've been trying to think of some creative way to tell you the news, but I'm just too befuddled to think of one."

"What 'news' are you talking about? You're not making sense, woman!" came the irritated response.

After a deep sigh Katie spoke quietly, "In about seven months I'm…no, we're going to have a baby."

Lucas sat speechless, trying to make sense of this new information. Katie held her breath, hoping to see some positive reaction. Instead, her husband seemed to grow cold. Without saying a word, he started the engine and pulled out into traffic. Both were silent the entire trip home.

Once at home Lucas left the car immediately and entered the house without waiting for Katie. She remained in the car trying to understand her husband's attitude. She had reacted with pure joy. Not only did she long for a little one she could shower with love, but she could also visualize that this event could bring her husband closer with their offspring as the common bond.

Confused and hurt, she slowly entered the house. A stern-looking Lucas met her at the door.

"I'll call Dr. Tom and have him locate a reputable clinic to take care of this situation." Lucas spoke abruptly.

"Take care of what situation?" Katie answered slowly. "What are you talking about? What are you trying to suggest?"

"Katlyn, surely you understand that this development is not what I brought you here for. This would only foul up everything. A quick abortion is the answer," Lucas stated firmly. "Besides, who is the father of your baby?"

Katie gasped in disbelief. "You are, of course. Why would you ask such a ridiculous question?"

In a menacing tone Lucas continued, "What is his name? Did you meet him while I was in Hawaii? Or does he come here under my own roof while I'm at the station?"

"Why would you say such horrible things? I have never given you any reason to doubt me. How could you even suggest that?" Katie could not fathom her husband's suspicions.

"Because I was married to Adrian for four years without a child, and now after less than five months of marriage you come up pregnant. What am I supposed to think?" he said accusingly.

"I have no idea why you had no children with Adrian, but I do know that you are the only man on earth that could be the father of this baby." Katlyn felt a burning anger rise from deep within her soul. She glared at her husband. When she spoke, her words were controlled yet powerful. With great conviction she continued slowly. "I will not murder the child I am carrying. If you wish me to leave you I will do so immediately, but be sure of one thing. This baby will live, and I will raise him. I never ever want to hear about an abortion again. The subject is closed!"

Stunned by his wife's obvious determination, Lucas watched her walk resolutely up the stairs, then he heard the door to her bedroom close firmly.

The next few weeks were extremely uncomfortable for the Lehmans. Katie knew her attitude was not pleasing to God, but she could not bring herself to be pleasant with the man who wanted to kill her baby. She continued to do her work but spoke very seldom. She did not forget her plan to show love to her husband, but she assumed God could never expect her to continue under these circumstances.

Lucas was also quiet and moody. Though he did not speak of it, he brooded constantly about how the entrance of a bawling brat would ruin his plans. Surely it would force them to evolve into a more traditional family, and that frightened him. He wanted Katie's explicit unquestioning obedience and her exclusive time and energy to be spent on his behalf. He felt as if he'd paid good money for that, and now he was being cheated. He had quickly abandoned the idea that Katie had been unfaithful to him and the child was not his but never let her know that this question had been resolved in his mind. Frankly, he wanted the mother-to-be to suffer as he was, so he was careful to do or say nothing that would make her more comfortable. In Lucas' mind, the one good thing that came out of this rotten situation was that this turn of events had stopped the warm responses his wife had shown since he came back from Hawaii. His plan to keep this a marriage without love was proceeding quite well, except for one detail. They were both extremely miserable.

This continued until a cool evening in October. Katie first noticed some slight bleeding and tried to convince herself it meant nothing. She went to bed early with no explanation to her husband. But she woke up when Lucas came to bed only to realize she was experiencing pain in her lower abdomen. She lay beside her sleeping husband trying to will the cramping to go away. Finally she slipped out and went into her room. She threw herself across the bed and began to beg God to make it stop. She was sure she was losing her baby. She wanted to wake Lucas and make him take her to the hospital, yet she didn't have the strength to face a refusal. She figured he'd want her to wait and make sure there was no chance to save the pregnancy. Confused and in pain, she continued to pray. At about 2:00 in the morning she noticed the little book one of the young women in the church back in Indiana had given her as a farewell gift. The paperback was the journal of a Christian lady that had been written in a German concentration camp during World War II. It included many Scripture verses that God had used to comfort and strengthen the dear Dutch woman. Now the same verses flooded Katie with comfort and hope as she endured her present affliction. She read and prayed and wept as she suffered through the waves of pain which came and went all night long.

As the sun began to come up in the morning, Katie was emotionally spent, but she had turned a spiritual corner. She knew there would be no baby born to her in the coming spring, but she also knew that some way somehow God would bring her through this trial, and she would again feel His joy.

When Lucas woke for work the next morning, he realized immediately that his wife was not beside him. Irritation swept over him. "I wondered how long it would be before she moved out of my bed and into her room," he thought. "Well, she's mistaken if she thinks I'll let this brat-to-be release her from our agreement or any of her duties. I paid dearly for this, and I deserve better in return."

With this attitude he stomped down the hall and unceremoniously threw open the door without knocking, but the sight of his wife drained all animosity from him. Katie was sitting up in bed with a Bible in her lap. Her eyes were swollen from crying; her face showed exhaustion, and her complexion was tinged with gray.

Lucas stood speechless as he tried to imagine what had happened. Katie spoke first in a tone that showed no emotion. "You don't have to worry anymore. There won't be any baby this spring."

Lucas stood motionless without making a sound. He couldn't comprehend what she was saying.

Recognizing his confusion she spoke plainly. "I've had a miscarriage."

Stunned by the news and the frail look of his young wife, Lucas was flooded with guilt and suddenly angry with his own selfishness. In that moment he realized what a tragedy this was for Katie, but he had no capacity to comfort her. Instead he blurted out angrily, "Why didn't you wake me up? Just trying to put the blame for all this on me, weren't you? Well, I'm not responsible for what I don't know. Don't you try to make me the bad guy. This wasn't my fault."

Katie only sighed and responded briefly, "No, Lucas. This wasn't your fault."

They met Dr. Tom at the emergency room where he confirmed Katie's diagnosis. She indeed had miscarried. He tried to reassure both prospective parents that there was probably nothing that could have been done. He encouraged them both that this in no way meant they would never have children. They should wait six months to a year and then try again.

As Katie was dressing to go home, Dr. Tom took Lucas aside and spoke quietly to him. "I'm really sorry for your loss, Lucas, but you're going to have to really help your wife at this time. She's liable to experience some depression in the next few weeks. Just be supportive. Let her know you still love her as much as ever. I'm especially concerned because

Katlyn seemed so ecstatic when I gave her the news, but I'm sure you'll be there for her. She's in good hands."

Lucas muttered something about doing his best as Katie rejoined them in the lobby. He mulled over the new circumstance as he silently drove Katie home. He truly was concerned about what grief would do to his wife. She had been so bold in defending the life of her unborn child – almost like a mother bear defending her cubs. How would she react now when her child had been stolen from her? What good could he do? He knew all too well how close to insanity grief could take a person, especially when he or she faces it alone, but he was sure that she could never accept his help since she knew he was relieved that there would be no baby in the spring. He was glad to forget the whole idea of his becoming a father… or was he?

The next few days were quiet as Katie was sternly ordered to rest while her husband clumsily attempted to wait on her. In spite of the pain of her loss, she had to smile at the awkward attempts of her mate to cook and keep up the housework. By the third day she couldn't take it anymore and arose early to start breakfast before Lucas woke up. He tried to firmly scold her for disobeying his orders, but he couldn't avoid hungrily devouring the ham and eggs, toast and fresh coffee she put before him.

After they finished their meal, she looked up to find her husband looking at her with concern. She quietly chuckled and said, "Now go back to work before you drive us both crazy."

He huffed and puffed a little about how she had to rest till she got her strength back, but he agreed that he was needed at the office if she could do without him. He was really glad to get away from the emotions filling the house. His concern for Katie's physical and emotional well being had made it difficult for him to concentrate on keeping his marriage void of affection. He sensed he'd better get back to work as soon as possible.

The rest of the week was heavenly for Katie. With explicit orders from her husband to do no work, she was free to pray and read the Word of God and write in her prayer journal. Even as her body grew stronger physically, the time spent with God began to heal Katie both spiritually and emotionally. By Friday Katie humbly accepted her loss as something permitted by her Heavenly Father. She once again trusted God to live His life through her so that she could again choose to love her husband. She couldn't quite imagine having the kind of loving relationship with her husband that she longed for, but it felt good to begin to hope again.

Lucas noticed with amazement the transformation in Katie. Even though he discovered her in tears a couple of times, she still seemed to have such peace. As he compared her experience with grief to his own, he recognized that she had an inner strength he did not have. This new awareness made him uneasy, so he decided he'd better renew his efforts to escape the emotional web that once again threatened to capture him. He constantly reminded himself to be wary of her charms, but it was more difficult this time. It was harder and harder to find fault with her. As soon as she sensed some way to please him, she employed it with great care. More and more he held that hated cologne container to relight the bitterness toward women and escape the temptation to care for Katie. He began manufacturing reasons to be angry with her. He felt he had triumphed when he saw that he had once again totally exasperated her, however it never lasted long. She would disappear for a while then return to whatever she was doing with her unperturbed manner.

CHAPTER 21

Lucas continued his undeclared war until one cold November afternoon. He had once again succeeded in leveling a cutting remark on his wife that shook her stamina and sent her upstairs again (to have a good cry, he assumed). This time he decided he was going to find out what she did up there. He tiptoed up the stairs just in time to see her close the door to her bedroom. "Just as I suspected," he thought, feeling cocky because he'd figured her out. To be sure he was accurate, he quietly turned the knob on her door and opened it a fraction of an inch. He expected to see her throw herself on her bed and bury her sobs in her pillow. What he did see was his wife quietly kneel at the side of her bed and begin moving her lips. He saw a tear run down her cheek, but he saw no anger in her countenance.

He suddenly felt rebuffed for the intentional wound he had given Katie. A sick feeling engulfed him as he noiselessly closed the door and retreated down the stairway.

His head hurt; his stomach churned; his eyes burned. In fact his whole body ached. He decided maybe he could overcome his discomfort if he went outside. The area had just had a winter storm the night before, and Lucas decided it might do him good to shovel the walkways and maybe shake off this sickening feeling.

He attacked the job with great vigor, but the harder he worked, the worse he felt. In spite of the cold, he felt as if he was burning up. Well, that made sense because of the physical activity, yet could this explain the dizziness that was coming over him? He tried to ignore it, but when he noticed the world around him beginning to grow dimmer, he decided he'd better get back in the house lest he pass out and Katie find him a few hours later frozen to death.

Panicked by this numbing weakness, he headed up the stairs toward help. Katie was shocked to look up from her prayers and see her husband stagger in almost as if he were drunk. She jumped up just in time to grab his arm and ease him down onto her bed. When she touched him fear struck her. He was burning up. She struggled to pull off his coat and boots. Then she immediately turned to the phone and called Dr. Tom at his residence. When Katie revealed Lucas' condition, Amy explained that her husband wasn't home but promised to page him. After she hung up the phone, Katie prayed for wisdom as she went to find a thermometer. His fever of just over 105 degrees terrified her. She coaxed Lucas into swallowing some fever reducing tablets, then she immediately began to bathe him with cool water. In his delirium he fought the cool wetness, but Katie persisted. It seemed as if it had been an eternity when she finally heard Dr. Tom's footsteps on the stairs an hour and a half later.

"Traffic was terrible," was all he said as he entered the room and started the examination of his friend.

"I think his fever has gone down a little since I called," Katie mumbled nervously as she watched the young doctor check her husband's vital signs.

After a thorough exam, Dr. Tom addressed Katie. "I've seen several patients with something like this over the last couple of weeks, but Lucas has an especially bad case. With this high fever I'd feel better if we put him in the hospital for observation.

A low almost growling, “No!” came from the occupant of the bed beside them.

“I don’t blame you a bit, Lucas, but I really believe this is a necessity,” Dr. Tom replied firmly.

“No,” the answer came louder.

“Hey listen, Old Pal, we need to do some tests and find out what’s causing this.”

Lucas wordlessly shook his head.

“But, Lucas, you don’t understand how serious this could be. Your fever could get dangerously high; there could be other complications. Lucas, I don’t want to scare you, but if this is what I suspect it is, there have been some fatalities from this virus. I really must insist you go to the hospital to get the care you need.

Again the stubborn response was negative. The reply was physically weak yet was full of inward resolve. “Katlyn will take care of me.” Then after a momentary pause, the question followed, “Won’t you?” Their eyes met, both tinged with fear. Lucas was afraid of rejection in his great weakness. Katie was overwhelmed with the fear of possible failure, recognizing her husband’s serious condition.

“All right,” Dr. Tom gave an exasperated consent. “We’ll try this one night and see how you’re doing tomorrow. Katie, come with me. I’ll give you complete instructions for taking care of that stubborn husband of yours tonight, but I’m afraid you won’t be getting much sleep.”

After the doctor was gone and Lucas fell into a fitful sleep, Katie poured out her heart to God at the bedside. It seemed so strange to see Lucas lying alone in her big bed. True, she had only slept there that first night, the days Lucas had been in Hawaii, and the night she had had her miscarriage; but this room was her haven, her respite from her husband’s periodic coldness and apparent dissatisfaction. She had felt safe in here because her husband seldom came into this room for any reason. Now he was here and didn't appear to be leaving any time soon.

As she prayed for strength and wisdom, her human frailty seemed magnified. She knew if anything happened to Lucas she would always feel responsible. She silently cried out in fear until she finally recognized she must be willing to trust God no matter what happened.

The night found her constantly awakened by the delirious ramblings of her husband. Not much that he said made sense, but occasionally she heard Adrian's name muttered in a higher disturbed pitch. She even heard God's name spoken as she continued to cool the burning skin. She wasn't sure the name was being petitioned or taken in vain, but it was spoken more than once.

As the sun was just peaking over the horizon, Lucas seemed to calm a little. Katie heard him quietly speak her name and thought he was conscious again and calling for her, but as she bent low to hear his request, she realized he was not awake, yet he quietly repeated her name over and over.

"Katie, Katie, Katie, Katie," he continued slowly but clearly.

It sounded very odd to Katie because she couldn't ever remember hearing him call her "Katie". When he used her name, he always said "Katlyn" in a very reserved manner. The sound of her name from his lips touched her, and she gently kissed his forehead. She had pulled a small couch over to his bedside earlier in the evening. She rested her head on the bed beside him, placed her hand gently on his arm, and fell into an exhausted sleep.

She had hoped to awake to see him smiling and over the crisis as one might see in a movie, but instead she awoke a couple of hours later to find him conscious but still extremely sick.

Dr. Tom's examination that afternoon found Lucas holding his own, but not really improving. After once again failing to convince his friend to enter a hospital, the doctor ordered Katie to bed for a couple of hours while he attended the patient. As she left the room, she grabbed her Bible from the bedside table. The doctor started to caution her to sleep — not read — but the words didn't come out. In that moment he realized this young woman needed something he couldn't supply or even prescribe. He also suspected she knew exactly how to obtain what she needed, while he, with all his education, did not. As she wordlessly left, he briefly pondered the idea that the book she held so purposefully might be the source of the inner strength that she so quietly displayed.

The next few days took all the physical strength Katie could muster. Many times she found herself tired, frightened, and frustrated...crying out to her Lord for help.

On the sixth day after the onset of Lucas' illness, Dr. Tom declared him to be out of danger and on the road to recovery. Three days after this declaration, Katie felt safe to leave her husband for a couple of hours to go to the grocery. Dr. Tom had picked up a few necessities for her, but she needed to do some major shopping to replenish their empty cupboards.

As she left, Lucas instructed her to get him some magazines, or he would go out of his mind with boredom. As he watched the car disappear down the driveway, Lucas looked around the room for something to distract him and pass the time. He picked up the Bible on the nightstand...the same Bible that Katie read at his bedside while she thought he was sleeping. He briefly leafed through the pages, but he put the book down quickly. That might be a nice crutch for his wife, but he wanted no part of it. He admitted that the woman who had been nursing him seemed to have something he did not, but he was not ready to admit he needed something. Well, maybe he did need "something", but not "religion". That was for women and weak men, not for him.

Still bored, he opened the drawer in the night stand and perused its contents. There were a few letters on top. He skimmed one from some friend named Patti. It was fluffy stuff about former friendships mixed in with stuff about Jesus. As he put the rose edged stationery back in the envelope, he considered the strange thought of Katie's life before she married him. For the most part he refused to entertain such thoughts. Lucas wasn't really comfortable thinking about his wife's former life, so he opened the next letter. This one also was full of churchy stuff that Lucas just couldn't stomach. As least he was pretty sure from these letters that the true facts about their marriage had been kept a secret.

The third letter was quite different and was apparently written by the brother in the armed services. There was a lot of small talk, some mush about being sorry and too much concern about how his sister was doing. It was obvious that her brother Mark knew something. Lucas wondered just how much he did know. He resented all the concern, as if he couldn't possibly make a woman happy. What right did this creep have to question her happiness? He just better mind his own business. Lucas couldn't afford some relative messing up his chances of continued advancement at the station. Maybe Lucas had better question his wife a little more closely about her brother.

When Lucas replaced the letters, he noticed a book in the bottom of the drawer. He opened it to find not printed pages but a woman's handwriting. A guilty feeling started to steal over him as he leafed through the book, but he pushed it aside with the thought that he'd put a lot of money into this arrangement, and he had every right to protect his assets any way he could, including reading his wife's journal. As he turned to the first page, he was surprised to find a small snapshot of himself. How did Katie come to have this picture, and why would she keep it in her diary? Puzzled by this discovery, he began to read.

Each entry was dated so Lucas could tell she started this journal shortly after they were married, but before she came to live with him. She wrote so openly he could immediately feel the struggle within her as she prepared to start her new life with him. He could also feel her disappointment and frustration when he had been so short tempered with her on the telephone the days before she moved north. He felt uncomfortable and irritated as he realized this wasn't a normal journal. It was more like an extremely long personal letter to God. The aggravation continued as he recognized he was practically the sole source of her great misery. He inwardly scoffed as she wrote about "all things work together for good" and about "making a choice to trust God to keep His promises."

"I wonder if she's figured out yet that all that rhetoric is a bunch of baloney," Lucas said out loud.

Equally disconcerting was Katie's description of her talk with her brother. She was asking God to help her brother Mark be able to forgive himself for something he had evidently done to his sister. Then she went on and on begging God to "reach" her brother.

Lucas skipped on ahead to the next entry which appeared to be the first night she entered his home. It was interesting to see her side of it. He had never really allowed himself to consider what a fearful undertaking this marriage arrangement had been for his young bride. On his part he had been excited to begin his fantasy as well as to impress Katie with his big house and intimidate her into cooperating with his calculated plan to win him his promotion. As he now read her assessment of that first day and then the next couple of weeks that were obviously tense and frustrating for Katie, he saw how difficult he had made the situation. Yet in spite of her fear and discouragement, one entry after another ended with an affirmation of God's goodness and a continuing hope for the future based on God's love.

Yes, Lucas was getting sick of reading about, "God, do this" and "please, God, help in this situation or that situation" and here was something about bad things working out for good. The woman was a real fanatic, and it made him quite uncomfortable, but not enough to put the journal down. In one entry she was asking God to let her go to church. In the next, she was asking for help for her tennis game.

He was just getting into the days he was in Hawaii when he heard the car in the driveway. He looked out the window just in time to see Katie pull the car into the garage. As he quickly skimmed over the next lines, he was annoyed to realize how much she had looked forward to his departure. Footsteps on the stairs forced him to deposit the journal at the bottom of the drawer just in time before Katie entered the room with a smile.

"How's my patient?" she greeted cheerfully.

"What took you so long?" came the quick retort, followed by the thought, "The reason she's so cheerful must be because she was so happy to get away from her sickly mean husband." The truth was that he really wished she'd stayed longer so he could have finished reading her journal. Yet that last bit of information he had read had soured his mood, and he took it out on Katie as usual.

Katie was fresh from precious time spent with her Savior as she drove back from the store, so she took his grumpiness in stride and responded with a smile, "I guess that means you missed me. Is there anything I can get you right now before I put all the groceries away?"

"The magazines I asked for, of course, before I die of boredom," he said, overly concerned that somehow his wife might suspect he had invaded her privacy. This statement about boredom would surely cover his tracks.

As she left to retrieve the reading material, he sighed in relief but immediately began trying to devise a way to safely return to the journal. He must think of some way to distract her so he could read in peace.

Lucas was unnerved when upon Katie's return with the magazines she suggested that he might be more comfortable in his own room. He flatly refused without much of an explanation. She was perplexed as to why he didn't want to go to his own bedroom, but there was no use arguing with him.

All Lucas was thinking was that if he left Katie's bedroom he'd never get the chance to read the rest of her journal. Somehow he had to get her out of the house again. Everything he thought of to ask her to go get for him, she had already thought of when she was out shopping.

As one day passed and then another, Lucas grew more impatient to return to Katie's writings. A couple of times he had tried sneaking it out while Katie was downstairs, but he highly feared if she caught him reading he would lose his chance to finish it forever, and his completion of the small volume had almost become the driving force of the now limited world of his sickbed. His growing irritation heightened his cross disposition, making life even more unbearable for Katie.

Katie had already noticed her own mental and emotional state was in a slow downward spiral. Though she didn't stop to ponder the reason for her growing despondency, it had begun in the fertile soil of exhaustion during the days and nights of constantly nursing her ailing husband. This came at a time when her body had not totally recovered from the miscarriage she had suffered only weeks before.

Lucas' presence at home every day all day had thrown her schedule off so she had been spending less and less time in prayer and in Bible study. In her weakened physical, emotional, and spiritual state, Katie had found it harder and harder to bounce back after her husband's sour attitude and vocal attacks. At a time when she needed God the most, she didn't feel like praying or reading God's Word. When she did force herself to turn to the Lord, she felt helpless and hopeless.

Lying in bed at night, she found herself pondering the last eight months of her life. She had faced so many difficulties during that time. Though sometimes it seemed God was helping her and there was hope for the future, at this point in her life she couldn't imagine her mate ever changing, except possibly for the worse. She thought about the Christmas season that was approaching. She had so looked forward to celebrating her Savior's birth with a genuine comprehension of why He came to earth, but how could she really do that with her husband's "bah, humbug," constantly echoing in her ear. Very gradually but surely the fingers of depression were surrounding her and tightening their grip. She missed her daily diet of Christian radio that had soothed and encouraged her in the previous weeks. The talks, verses, and sermons taught her as a young believer things she was missing because her husband refused to allow her to attend church. Since Lucas' illness, Katie had often drifted off to sleep while reading the Bible or praying. With Lucas in her bedroom, she had only written in her prayer journal briefly when she was sure he was asleep. She never stopped to analyze what was happening. She just felt herself drying up on the inside and weakening with no understanding of why.

Chafed by the continuing desire to invade the secret thoughts of his wife, Lucas finally devised a plan he was convinced would give him the time he needed to read.

Saturday evening when Katie brought his meal, Lucas spoke abruptly, "I don't want you to make a habit of this, but I've decided you need to get out of the house for a while, so you can go to church tomorrow."

He waited for some gushy grateful response, but Katie stood speechless, just staring at him. After a few moments of silence, he continued. "Well, if you don't want to go, that's fine with me, but don't..."

"Oh, no!" Katie interrupted. "I'd really love to, I just didn't...I mean I was...that is, I never expected you to..."

"Stop blubbering and go get me some ketchup," Lucas cut in, "or I'm liable to change my mind."

Katie was still shaking her head in disbelief as she left the house Sunday morning. Lucas had insisted she stop and eat out after church and then go Christmas shopping before she came home. He had even shown her a picture of the brief-case he had instructed her to give him for Christmas. He also matter-of-factly suggested she look at jewelry because that was what he intended to buy her for Christmas as soon as he was back on his feet. She smiled to herself as she recalled that her husband had seemed embarrassed when he realized she had no jewelry the thieves had considered worth stealing.

The moments passed slowly to Lucas as he impatiently waited to hear the car in the driveway. At last he felt safe to retrieve the journal from the bedside table. He decided to go downstairs for the first time since his illness and read the journal in the den. He had wanted to start getting up more for a few days now, but he knew that once Katie realized he was well enough to be up and around, he'd have no more excuse to remain in her bedroom. Hopefully his ingenuity would give him enough time to read the journal in its entirety.

Quickly finding where he had left off, he re-entered Katie's private world. As he consumed page after page, he was bombarded with conflicting emotions. One moment he was angry because she had gone to church while he was in Hawaii. The next moment he was feeling guilty realizing the struggle his wife experienced because she had not been around other people since their marriage. Her excitement over some book about living a "victorious" Christian life (whatever that could be) was beyond his comprehension. Yet even though he had no understanding of the concepts she was recording, he felt as if he was becoming acquainted with a new person. The woman who had shared her inmost being in these pages had an inner depth to which Lucas had been totally oblivious until now.

He was instantly furious as he mentally searched the attic with her for a photo so she could concentrate on learning to love her husband. It was both insulting and frightening. When he was in high school and college, Lucas had prided himself with his ability to charm the ladies. He always knew what to say to make a girl feel good. Katie had never experienced his charisma, only his pride and his rebuffs. Part of him wanted to turn on his charms toward his wife. He wished he could prove to her how irresistible he could be. It was aggravating to comprehend that his pretty bride had to try to force herself to love him.

He had truly felt the effects of her love those weeks after Hawaii. Her sweet attention was what kept him battling to accomplish the loveless existence he hoped to maintain. Or was it really love he had felt? Was it all just an act? Could someone really learn to love someone who returned only coolness and reproof as he had done to her so consistently? As he pondered the thought uncomfortably, he decided that if anyone could, it would surely be his determined wife, especially since she seemed to have a partnership with the Almighty.

As he continued to daydream, he considered Katie's confrontation with his first wife by way of pictures and the video. He had never wanted Katie to know anything about Adrian. Honestly, the only time he allowed himself to think about her was when he felt himself drawn to his new wife. To counteract his growing weakness, he would force himself to remember the pain Adrian had put him through. At those times he would pick up the bottle of men's cologne he had retrieved from Adrian's bedroom. The half used bottle that had to have belonged to her lover brought thoughts that never failed to rekindle his anger and hatred so he could fend off all feelings that threatened to entangle his heart. At the same time it seemed ridiculous for Katie to imagine he still loved his first wife when he despised her memory so. Maybe it was for the best for Katie to think that. He didn't know.

Katie's description of the burglary sent Lucas into another reverie of those days gone by. He remembered the fear that had coursed through him. Not just the fear of losing his promotion or even his fantasy, but he remembered too well that sudden fear of losing her companionship. Even now he was fighting the idea as he continued to ponder the past. He relived that moment when their eyes met at the airport. He had mixed emotions now after learning that her changed attitude hadn't been the result of their separation. It wasn't that she had missed him as he had supposed. No, she had made a decision to love him after reading a book. This was certainly a bit hard on his ego. As he read on about their night out with the boss and his wife, he recognized genuine love in her words. Even with his daily rebuffs, she continued to show more depth of love; that is until the pregnancy. Then suddenly he saw a different love emerge and grow. It was a love for the baby she carried.

"How could she love a child she's never seen?" Lucas wondered.

Yet the love was obvious. Just as obvious was Katie's struggle with her emotions toward her husband. Her mother's instincts rose up against the one man on earth who wanted to kill her baby. Caught up in her writing, Lucas found himself siding with Katie. He couldn't blame her for her inability to stir up love for her husband.

When he at last came to the record of the night Katie lost the baby, Lucas read with a lump in his throat. He felt her anguish as she said goodbye to her unborn child. In the back of his mind he realized for the first time that it was his loss, too.

In the pages that followed, Lucas saw once again this young woman emerge from her private turmoil and recover emotionally from it. Lucas sighed in unbelief as Katie once again returned to her mission — that is to love her unloving husband.

Then all of a sudden, he read the last written page. The rest of the journal was blank. The last notation had been written as she sat at his bedside some nights ago. He once again felt her love as she desperately prayed for him. The strange part of this last page was that she seemed more concerned about his spiritual health than his physical health. She was pleading with God to keep him alive until he accepted Jesus' forgiveness and received the gift of salvation.

Lucas felt as if there was a war raging inside him. On one hand, thoughts came to him like, "Forgiveness for what? How dare she portray me as some sinner! What have I done that is so evil? How dare she complain about the life I've provided for her? She has a beautiful home, a successful husband, her every need met!"

Yet another thought countered, "What had he really ever given to her beyond the material needs. He'd certainly never given himself or love or friendship or understanding or sympathy or encouragement or even a kind word. Had he ever given her anything of true importance? So how was it she could still even consider loving him? He'd heard about women who had stayed with cruel and abusive husbands instead of leaving them. Was there something about some women that kept them trapped in a bad situation? He'd seen a documentary about that once. Yet all those women seemed to have a false idea that they couldn't hope for more out of life or didn't deserve more or something like that.

Katie was unlike any woman he had ever known. In spite of all his calculated attempts to bully her into submission to his plan of a platonic marriage, it was clear she hadn't bought the idea. Though on the outside she appeared totally submitted to his control as a husband, from what he had just read she was totally free of any psychological control. What gave her this inner strength? Could it be that there was something to this "God thing" she obviously believed? Was there really a God out there at all? If there was, did He really care about individuals and what went on in their daily lives? If God did care so much, how could He have allowed horrible things to happen...like his own tragic marriage. Lucas had to admit that Katie had something that he didn't. He might even admit that he'd really like to have it. He felt so empty inside most of the time.

Wait. What was this written in the back cover of the journal? At the top the printing was underlined.

What I learned the night I met Jesus Christ

1. I John 5:13 "I write these things to you who believe in the name of the Son of God so that you may know that you have eternal life." *Explanation: You can know for sure that you are going to heaven.*
2. Romans 3:23 "For all have sinned and fall short of the glory of God." *Explanation: Everyone who's ever lived has done wrong and doesn't measure up to God's standard.*
3. Romans 6:23 "For the wages of sin is death, but the gift of God is eternal life in Christ Jesus our Lord." *Explanation: The payment I deserve for the sins I have done is death forever in Hell. (Mrs. Rice said Hell is a real place. Heaven is also a real place, but going there is a gift.)*
4. Ephesians 2:8, 9 "For it is by grace you have been saved, through faith—and this not from yourselves, it is the gift of God — not by works, so that no one can boast." *Explanation: As the last verse said, I can't do anything to be good enough to go to heaven. But I must have faith. That is I must believe that Jesus*

died for my sins on the cross so they could all be forgiven.

5. Acts 20:21 "I have declared to both Jews and Greeks that they must turn to God in repentance and have faith in our Lord Jesus Christ." *Explanation: To repent is not just asking God to forgive you for your sins. It means that you are willing to change your attitude toward God and turn from sin.*

   The prayer Mrs. Rice suggested that I say to Jesus: "Lord Jesus, I ask that you forgive me for sinning. I don't want to sin anymore. Come into my life and be my Savior and my Lord. Thank you for dying on the cross for my sins."

I prayed this prayer in May, and my life hasn't been the same since that evening.

As Lucas pondered Katie's account of this experience, he briefly considered the possibility that there was any validity to what she had recorded. Negative thoughts soon flooded his mind. This kind of thing was only for weak-minded people who needed a crutch to get through life. Katie had probably been pushed into this by whatever wicked or stupid thing she had done that also brought her to agree to marry a stranger.

Suddenly he wondered how long he'd been sitting there. He had a panicky feeling that his wife would come home and catch him reading her journal. He felt tired...physically, mentally, and emotionally. He trudged up the stairway and gently placed the book into the bedside drawer. He felt almost melancholy, realizing he might never again be able to enter the world of Katie's private thoughts.

Lucas then became conscious of how tired and physically weak he was. He silently cursed the microscopic demons that had attacked his body so successfully. Yet he was determined to accomplish one more task before he returned to his sickbed. He dreaded the thought, but he felt compelled to go up to the attic. Christmas was almost here, and somehow he thought he owed it to Katie to get the decorations down for her. He had no desire to celebrate anything right now, but he assumed his wife would want that.

Lucas had not been in the attic for years — not since he had deposited all of Adrian's belongings up there in a heap. He remembered that day as a time of intense grief, bitterness, and hatred. As he ascended the stairs to the attic, he felt almost numb. The pain of past days was almost gone, and the hatred was more of a disgusted dislike. Could the old adage "time heals all wounds" be true; or could Katie's presence in his house have lessened the pain? Maybe he was just too tired to feel anything because of his illness. Whatever the reason, he made several trips up and down the stairs to retrieve the Christmas decorations that had not been used since Adrian's death. Only once did he look over at the pile of feminine clothing. A sickening feeling washed over him, but he willed himself to return to his task.

Once back into his own bed in his own room, he began to ponder his new situation. Deep inside he knew his attitude toward Katie would never be the same again. It was as if he'd peered deep into her soul, and he couldn't deny an admiration for her character. Somehow he must stay aloof. Maybe it was true that some of his past pain had dulled, but he struggled to maintain his determination to never love another woman. Yet as he drifted off to sleep, his last thought was, "Even a woman like Katie."

CHAPTER 22

As Katie drove home later that afternoon, she pondered her day out. She smiled as she remembered the warm welcome she had received at the little church she revisited. Many even remembered her name. As she had sat in the pew soaking in both the spiritual teaching as well as the loving atmosphere, she had wondered how long it would be until she could return. She strongly suspected that Lucas did not intend this to be a regular Sunday happening. She had no idea what brought about this change of heart, but she praised God for the opportunity.

The afternoon had passed quickly as she hurriedly ate a lunch then did her Christmas shopping. She had found the briefcase her husband had requested in the second store she looked in, so she had time to browse, looking for some "surprises" for her mate. She was a bit uneasy about trying to choose things that would please Lucas. Many times she wondered if she would ever please him. It seemed that his approval was always just out of reach.

She did feel somewhat confident about one choice. She had noticed a small travel sized bottle of men's cologne in her husband's bedroom. The small container always seemed to be out as if had just been used, yet it had remained less than half full since she noticed it several months ago. She reasoned that he used it only on special occasions or else it would have been completely gone long ago. She really loved the fragrance and was excited to find a bottle that looked identical, but in a larger size. She wasn't sure of her other choices…the sweater or the tie…but at least she found a fragrance he obviously liked.

Katie's thoughts turned to spiritual matters. Sitting in church a few hours earlier listening to the pastor's encouraging words, she had come to a realization. In the seven months that she had been married she had never once talked to Lucas about his spiritual condition. In fact, even now she couldn't imagine bringing up the subject. She was sure his response would be negative…maybe quietly menacing or maybe loudly abusive…but it would surely be negative. How could it possibly help to even bring up the subject of Jesus? Yet she was equally sure about something else. She didn't want her husband to go to Hell. Though it was apparent to her that Lucas did not love her, she truly did care about him, and she did want him to come to know Jesus personally. How anyone could get through to a man like her husband, she had no idea. Somehow she had to try.

Her mind shifted easily into a prayer. "Lord, I'm sorry I've never said anything to Lucas about You. I won't make excuses. I guess I've been a coward. Help me to open my mouth. Show me what I should say. Could You somehow tap him on the shoulder and work on him for me? I don't have any idea what to say or how to say it. So just please help me."

The first things Katie spotted as she entered the house were five boxes neatly marked X-MAS stacked at the bottom of the stairs. She cautiously opened the top box to make sure the contents matched the labeling. She lifted the lid to find carefully wrapped delicate ornaments. Smiling through tears, Katie whispered a heartfelt "thank you" to God. She had wondered what to do about decorating for the holidays, but Lucas' ill health had kept her from asking him about what he wanted.

Suddenly she realized that these boxes had been in the attic which must have required several trips up and down two flights of stairs. When she left, she thought her husband was barely able to walk across the floor. She hurried up to her room to check on the invalid but found only an empty bed.

Somewhat puzzled and with a growing uneasiness, she walked downstairs, checking each room and finding each room unoccupied. Next she tried the little den in the basement, but to no avail. She moved slowly up the stairs, pondering the situation. Where could he have gone?

"Dear Lord Jesus," she began uncertainly. "I know this sounds silly, but I seem to have lost my husband. He's been so sick, and I was gone so long; I'm really worried. Now that I've admitted it, I remember that there is something in the Bible about not worrying and praying about things instead of just worrying. So, God, could you please help me find Lucas? Please show me where he is."

As she headed back toward her bedroom, it suddenly occurred to her that she had not looked in her husband's bedroom. The only reason she had been in there since Lucas became ill was to get him clean pajamas and underwear. Opening the door quietly, she felt a mixture of relief and embarrassment.

"Sorry, Lord," she thought silently. "I feel really stupid, but thanks for helping me anyway."

Lucas was sleeping so soundly, Katie decided to use this opportunity to wrap her gifts and do a little decorating. She lovingly wrapped each gift, trying to imagine her spouse's reaction when he opened them. She was finally looking forward to Christmas...the first Christmas since she had received the ultimate gift...the gift of salvation. This was the first year that she understood the meaning of Christmas, the reason that God's Son came to earth over 2000 years ago.

After hiding her newly-wrapped gifts in the laundry room, she began to peruse the decorations. Just as she was opening the third box, she heard her name called from upstairs. She scurried up the steps so quickly she was out of breath when she reached Lucas' bedside.

"How are you feeling this afternoon?" Katie said cheerfully.

"Like a Mack truck ran over me," he replied sourly.

"Well, I'm not surprised. You've barely been out of bed for over two weeks and your first time up you decide to go up and down two flights of stairs several times. Why didn't you wait for me to get the decorations down?"

"Because I didn't want to wait," was his only defense. "Go find me something to eat while I call some place up and have them deliver a Christmas tree."

"But Lucas, don't you think we should wait till you're a little stronger? I don't want you to get overtired and have a relapse."

"Don't worry. When I get tired, I'll just direct you from the sofa."

And that's exactly what he did. Katie felt awkward and unsure of herself under his watchful eye as she attempted to find the perfect place for each of the beautiful ornaments and decorations. Wherever she went she could feel his eyes on her. She had learned a long time ago that if her husband was in the mood to talk, he would start the conversation. If he wasn't in the mood, nothing she could say would change that. Tonight he apparently wasn't in the mood because he was reclining on the sofa, not speaking a word, and watching her every move with an unreadable expression on his face.

Lucas, on the other hand, was having more fun than he'd had in years. He purposely maintained the dead pan look as he attempted to see the woman he had met in the journal.

He recognized her uneasiness and also realized that he had prevented her from being herself…from being that strong yet caring person he had come to know in the pages of the book. Tonight it was as if he was being introduced to a new person. This was the first time he had ever really tried to see her for who she really was.

It was true that what he was doing this very moment was exactly what he had carefully avoided from the beginning. He felt as if he'd opened Pandora's box and let the secret out, and now he couldn't resist trying to see more of the real Katie.

Katie's frustration grew under Lucas' silent stare until she fumbled a delicate ornament, letting it fall onto a lamp table shattering into dozens of pieces.

"Oh, Lucas, I'm so sorry. How clumsy of me. That was such a beautiful ornament, too," Katie moaned.

Lucas, however, recognized immediately that the destroyed object had been Adrian's favorite.

"Good riddance," was his terse reply.

As Katie left the room to get a broom and dustpan to clean up the shattered glass, she began to think about her new determination to share Jesus Christ with her husband. She suddenly had an idea of how she might approach the subject.

"You know, Lucas, there is one more decoration I'd like to get to complete our festive new look around here," Katie tried to say lightly as she swept up the broken glass. "We don't seem to have a nativity set and since this is the first Christmas that I've actually understood what the holiday is all about, I'd really like to display the manger scene."

"What in the world do you mean, you understand what the holiday is all about?" Lucas snapped with a definite undertone of sarcasm.

"Well," Katie proceeded slowly, recognizing the tone in her husband's voice. "It's a little hard to explain. You see …

all my life I enjoyed all the Christmas traditions—the tree, the lights, Santa, Rudolph, Frosty the Snowman, and even the nativity scene, but I never understood how a baby born in a stable fit in with all the other holiday celebrations."

"And now you do understand?" Lucas interrupted skeptically.

Katie laughed nervously as she tried to phrase her words so they made sense. "To be perfectly honest, I still don't understand how they all fit together, but what I do realize now is why that baby came to Bethlehem that first Christmas night."

Katie paused momentarily and glanced at her husband, unsure how he was responding to the subject, but she couldn't read his expression. The truth was that Lucas was very uncomfortable. For the first time since Adrian's death, he had let his guard down. He had actually just relaxed as he watched his wife walk around his home, recognizing her beauty…not so much on the outside (though he did find her attractive), but more so her inner beauty. Then in this weak moment, out of the blue, she springs this on him. Something was telling him to silence her before she said any more, but another part of him wanted to hear her answer. So he just stared, making no response.

Katie broke the brief silence as she continued. "Until last spring I never knew that the birth of Jesus was part of a carefully laid out plan. God's Son had to be born, live a perfect life, and then die on a cross and be punished by God for everyone's sins. Then He arose from the grave and went back up to heaven with His Father."

"And what, may I ask, does all that have to do with anything going on in this house tonight?" Lucas barked.

Determined to make her point, Katie continued, "Well, last spring, shortly after we were married, I realized for the first time that I could never be good enough to please God or to go to heaven some day. At the same time I found out that

Jesus had taken all my sins on the cross and paid the penalty that I deserved. All I had to do was to accept for myself what He did on the cross...like accepting a gift. So I did take that gift and ever since then, Jesus has been in my life guiding me and helping me."

After another awkward silence, Lucas replied. "Katlyn, buy your nativity set. Spend as much as you like. But next time just spare me the sermon."

Without another word, he left the room, going straight up to his bed. Katie sat numbly wondering if this first witness to her husband had gone well. It appeared he was hard as a rock, but she still thanked the Lord for the opportunity. She would continue to pray for what seemed impossible...that Lucas would come to know Jesus as she did.

Lucas, though he had not shown it, was inwardly shaken. The only thoughts of God he'd had for the last several years were angry thoughts blaming God for the suffering he had experienced. That was until he read Katie's journal. To confront this God on the printed page had been disarming enough, but now to hear about Him from Katie's soft compelling voice was affecting him deeply. When she talked about God, it seemed as if He was real, and she was personally acquainted with Him. One thing Lucas was sure of, though, was that if he embraced Katie's way of thinking, the wall of protection he had carefully built to guard his emotional well-being would be permanently shattered.

CHAPTER 23

The next days passed quickly as Lucas improved and started back to work. Katie found the perfect manger scene to which she gave a prominent place on the great room mantle above the fireplace. Lucas made no comment, but he observed when Katie was out of the room how real the tiny characters seemed. The tiny baby surrounded by hay, the young woman seated beside the manger, the bearded man peering over her shoulder, and the adoring shepherds bowing before the child. It struck him odd that grown men would be groveling before a newborn baby. Just as he began to ponder the thought, Katie entered the room and he forced his mind to think on other things.

A war was raging in Lucas' mind. Could he be approaching some sort of breakdown? At times Katie's words, both verbal and from her journal, would come to him. As he pondered her quiet assertions, he would be attacked with ugly thoughts and feelings from the past. Adrian's face would suddenly come to his memory followed by pain, then hatred unlike he'd felt for many months. He'd even considered seeking professional advice, but his pride wouldn't let him admit to anyone that he needed help. He tried to tell himself it was just the aftermath of the serious illness he was recovering from and as soon as his body was stronger, his mind would recover.

Over the next couple of weeks Katie sensed something was wrong as her husband wavered from almost congenial to short-tempered and moody to displaying fiery outbursts. She continued to pray more and more diligently for him to understand the truth about Jesus.

Lucas spent much time going from jewelry store to jewelry store, trying to find that perfect piece of jewelry to give his wife for Christmas. He wanted to spend a decent amount of money on the gift, but the larger pieces seemed gaudy when he thought of Katie's fragile neck. Finally he found a necklace that seemed fitting. It was a finely-crafted heart, decorated with diamonds on a delicate gold chain. Though he couldn't understand why this gift was so important to him, at least it was taken care of, and he could relax until Christmas.

Finally the special day came. Lucas decided they would open their gifts on Christmas Eve, mostly because Adrian had always been adamant about waiting until Christmas morning to celebrate, though he was careful not to explain his reasons to Katie. First they went out for an early dinner at a cozy little restaurant he knew would still be open on Christmas Eve. It began to snow as they drove home, and, at Lucas' request, they sat in the driveway, watching the large flakes quickly blanket the ground.

Katie was thankful for the peaceful moments. The last days had been extremely uncomfortable with Lucas' moods. She had almost dreaded the holiday. She briefly closed her eyes and breathed a silent prayer for her husband and for their coming evening together. She so wanted it to be the perfect Christmas. Her thoughts moved to the first Christmas and what a difference that humble birth had made in her existence these last months. How could she have endured the emotional uncertainties without the friendship of God? Looking up suddenly, Katie realized that her husband was no longer watching the snowy scene but was watching her with a puzzled half grin. Both were suddenly uncomfortable and moved in unison to make their way back to the house. Katie headed for the kitchen to fix some hot chocolate while Lucas started a fire in the big, but rarely used fireplace. By the time Katie came in with their warm brew, the fire was dancing merrily in the hearth, projecting a warm glow throughout the room. Lucas decided to leave the glass guard open so they could enjoy the full effect and warmth of the flames. The pine scent from the festive tree completed the effect.

Sitting on the luxurious sofa, Katie watched as her spouse brought the presents from under the tree. She longed to feel truly at home, but that continual edge of uneasiness was the couple's constant companion. They each had four gifts to open. Lucas first handed her a professionally wrapped package containing a pricey designer dress he hoped would fit her. His emotions began to swell as he read the genuine appreciation in her eyes.

Next he opened the sweater Katie had chosen and immediately slipped it on over his shirt to show his approval. They both were keeping their favorite for last. For Lucas it was the necklace. He hoped she would realize its value. Katie held back the cologne, hoping it would be a delightful surprise.

Lucas watched Katie's face as she finally opened the delicate necklace. The warmth and love in her response was all Lucas could have hoped for. As she looked up to say thank you, she was startled by the expression on her husband's face. For the first time ever she thought she could almost detect love in his eyes. He looked, at the moment, as if he truly cared for her.

What Lucas noticed was a teardrop slip from her eyelash and touch her cheek. Suddenly worried, he quickly asked, "Is something wrong? Are you disappointed? Don't you like the necklace?"

"No, Lucas," Katie answered with a soft voice. "I don't just like it. I really really adore it. And I really love..."

Now she struggled for control. She felt so much like putting her love into words, but she was afraid of ruining the moment. After hesitating she continued softly, "I really do love the necklace. Would you put it on for me?"

As Lucas fumbled clumsily with the tiny chain, the thought came to his mind that in spite of all of his past efforts, this small heart of gold and diamonds represented his own heart. The self control he'd been striving so hard to maintain weakened steadily as he finally closed the clasp.

Uncomfortable with the emotionally charged atmosphere, Lucas picked up his last gift and sat down beside Katie to open it. She sat in quiet anticipation, hoping for his approval. Instead he responded with only a blank expression. As Lucas pulled the bottle from the gift box, he slowly stood just staring at the bottle of cologne, letting the shiny wrappings fall to the floor. Standing silently in front of the fire, he fingered the bottle for what seemed to Katie an eternity. Then suddenly without warning, he hurled the bottle into the fire as a single word of rage filled the room. The word "why" mixed with the noise of broken glass as the bottle shattered on the grating of the fireplace. The liquid ignited into a miniature inferno, then disappeared as suddenly as it came, wafting an eerie perfumed scent throughout the room.

"I'm so sorry, Lucas," Katie began apologizing. "What have I done? I thought you'd like the cologne. I figured it was a favorite since you always keep it sitting out on your dresser. It's the same kind in that little bottle upstairs. Please forgive me. I didn't mean any harm..."

Her voice trailed off as her husband disappeared up the stairs into his bedroom flinging the door shut with a crash that echoed in Katie's ears. Next came the horrible silence. Katie sat in shock...motionless...wondering what she had done and what she should do now. From deep within, an agonizing feeling of utter hopelessness welled up. As despair began to totally overwhelm her, she began to sob uncontrollably. She buried her face in the couch pillows to muffle the sound of her agony. As tears flowed unchecked, thoughts of the last few depressing months crowded her mind. Before her memory raced failure after failure after failure after failure to win her husband's affection. She saw all her many attempts and recalled how each had been so dismally received. Then tonight had seemed so special. She had been so full of hope, but somehow she had spoiled it all. Somehow that bottle of cologne that was meant to draw them closer together had smashed the fragile emotions of the evening and decimated all of Katie's hope for the future.

In the midst of her despair she found herself talking to her Heavenly Father which had become her natural response to disappointment, but this was the lowest she had ever been.

"I give up, Lord," she began. "No matter what I do, my husband rejects me. And now I've made some stupid blunder that has made him hate me even more. I feel so sorry and so responsible for causing him pain. Maybe that cologne was Adrian's last gift to Lucas, and it brings back haunting memories. I can't think of any other possible explanation.

"And, Lord, I feel so utterly defeated. How could I have allowed myself to think my marriage could be happy and loving? My husband will never love me. He'll probably never even like me. I might as well be realistic about my future instead of hoping against hope and then being crushed every time the truth lifts its ugly head."

She paused for a few moments, trying to control her sobbing and make herself face reality. Then out loud she whispered huskily into her pillow, "I just can't do it, Lord. I just can't hope any more. I'm too tired, and it hurts too much. Forgive me. I quit."

Then for what seemed a long time she just sat, trying not to think. Yet other thoughts came to war against those to which she had succumbed. They brought words of comfort and promise. At first she felt they mocked her. "All things work together for good." "I can do everything through him who gives me strength." "I will never leave you nor forsake you." "Apart from me you can do nothing." "I will be with him in trouble."

It didn't really feel as if these statements were true...not right now anyway. Yet something within her challenged her to believe it anyway. She remembered that her pastor's wife had said that you should make a choice *not* to believe your feelings and then make a choice to believe God.

"Okay, God," she finally breathed. "I choose to trust you. Here's my life. Do whatever you want."

Katie lifted her head and was startled to see Lucas standing beside her just watching. She felt awkward...unsure of what to say.

"Lucas," she began slowly. "I'm sorry I hurt you. I had no idea..."

"Katie," the somber man interrupted as if he had not heard her speaking. "We have to talk."

This simple statement threw Katie's mind into turmoil. On the one hand, his tone was quiet, not foreboding. Except for in his delirium, her husband had never called her "Katie"...only "Katlyn."

On the other hand, he seemed so serious and after what had just happened with the cologne, she feared he was about to announce that the marriage wasn't working and that he planned to dissolve it early before the year had passed. She bit her lip for control as he sat at the other end of the sofa and turned to face her.

"First of all, I want to know what it was that forced you to agree to this marriage. I never asked before because I didn't really want to know. But I do now. So if you don't mind, please tell me everything," Lucas ended his calm plea.

Katie paused, trying to decide where to begin, wondering what was behind Lucas' request. "I guess it started with my parents' deaths. They died in an auto accident nearly three years ago now. That's when I came to feel responsible for my younger brother Mark. After he had been in college for a couple of years, I thought he was doing fine, until Joe showed up and told me Mark owed his "employer" $25,000 in gambling debts, and we had only a short time to pay up or there would be serious consequences. Since Mark had already been severely beaten the week before, I feared the worst, but I had nowhere to turn for the money; no close relatives to confide in; no credit history to make me a good risk for a loan that large. The crazy marriage 'proposal' seemed like an answer to prayer, though until all of this started happening, I'd never done much praying."

When Katie finally found the courage to glance over at Lucas, he looked sick as he slowly shook his head. He was mumbling something, apparently to himself. "She gives up her future and marries a perfect stranger to get her kid brother out of trouble. Now I'm supposed to tell her my side of this proposition. Do I dare tell her everything?"

Then he looked her in the face and said bluntly, "So that's all there was to it. You married me to save your brother's neck. What kind of brother would let you do something so outrageous?"

"He wanted to stop me, but there was no other alternative. This was the only way to get the money quickly enough. It was my decision, not his," she defended. "Why did you think I agreed to marry you anyway?"

"I don't know what I thought, and frankly, I tried not to think about it. I just figured you'd done something bad or at least incredibly stupid, and you were just getting what you deserved. I never anticipated anything like this. It sure makes my story harder to tell."

"Then just don't tell it," Katie started, but Lucas cut her off with a firm, "No, you have to know the whole truth. Then we'll see how you feel about your husband."

Lucas began with his romance and marriage to Adrian. He included all the details as he chronicled his four year marriage, hoping they would help Katie understand. When he was relaying the horror of finding out about both the death of his beloved and the proof of her infidelity all in one day, he glanced at his wife long enough to see tears in her eyes. Yet he couldn't look as he told the next chapter of hatred and bitterness which ended with his fantasy of convenience to insure his promotion and run his household.

He dared not look as he continued to reveal his war to keep their marriage totally platonic…void of emotion.

"And I might have succeeded if it hadn't been for that journal," he offered.

"My prayer journal?" Katie whispered in disbelief.

"Yes," Lucas responded in a low voice. "I know it was very wrong, but I honestly can't say I'm sorry I read it."

"But how? When?" was all Katie could say.

"When I was sick in your room…while you were at the store and then the day you went to church. I started reading it because I was so utterly bored; but after only a few pages, I was hooked. I felt as if I was peering into your very soul, and I wanted to know everything. After I had worked so hard to keep our relationship shallow and unemotional, I came to see you more intimately than anyone but God Almighty.

"I thought after this revelation that I could go right back to our former aloof marriage, but something had changed. When I tried to use my temper and moods to distance us, I couldn't make it last. Even that little bottle of 'his' cologne couldn't rouse my anger for long."

Lucas looked over to see Katie's eyes opened wide with understanding and horror. "Yes, that cologne belonged to Adrian's lover. She had the nerve to bring him into my own home to carry on her disgusting relationship. I found that travel-sized bottle in her bedroom the day that I buried her, and I kept it in my room as a constant visible reminder to never trust a woman again. When I opened that gift tonight, I felt as if a war was raging inside of me. Part of me wanted to hate you and all women for my past pain; and part of me was angry because I was on the verge of admitting to myself that maybe you're not like the Adrians of the world…and the cologne reminder was pushing us apart."

"That's not the only battle, though. Your journal introduced me to Someone else, too. The way you talked to God on those pages sounded as if you actually knew Him personally. Yet something inside of me had to reject that because if He's such a wonderful friend, then why did He let me go through these years of nightmare. It would be emotionally stabilizing to believe God cared about us, but it just didn't fit my experience. So back and forth I went as the war continued in my mind. Then just now, upstairs in my room, two things became very clear to me. The first is that you have something that I don't have, and I want it. Listen, I know God must be the key to whatever it is that makes you different from anyone else I've ever known, but how did you come to know Him as you do?"

Katie was stunned. This was the last thing in all the world she expected to hear from her husband tonight. Her thoughts were thrown into a jumble. She hesitated, not sure where to begin.

Lucas misread her hesitancy and continued apologetically. "I know I have a lot of nerve asking you to help me after all I've put you through these last months. I wouldn't blame you if you never spoke to me again. I know I don't deserve it. A man has to be pretty low to do to a woman what I've done to you. I'm so miserable. Just tell me what I have to do."

"Of course, I'll tell you," Katie encouraged, "but I've never done this before. I mean I've never told anyone how Jesus can become his Savior. I'm just trying to think about where to begin."

"What about your journal?" Lucas offered hesitantly.

Katie was baffled. "My journal?" she questioned.

Lucas clarified meekly. "Well, I'm ashamed to bring it up again, but in the back cover of your journal you have some verses written. Would that help?"

"Oh yes, Lucas. I'd forgotten about that. Let me go get it."

Her knees were shaky as she made her way up the stairs to retrieve her journal and her beloved Bible from the drawer in her bedside table. Suddenly her mind was flooded with all the negative things she had said about her husband in her writing. How could she face him after all he had read? Katie began to pray for help to forget all that, so she could think clearly. She was so nervous that she would say the wrong thing and Lucas wouldn't understand or worse yet that she would bungle the conversation, and he would reject God's gift of salvation. She truly loved this man and wanted him to know her Savior personally as she did.

In the dim light of the fire Lucas had rekindled, Katie shared the verses about sin and its results, about the cross and how Jesus took our punishment when He died there. In simple humility, Lucas confessed his sinfulness and asked Jesus Christ to become his Savior and Lord.

"God," he began slowly, pausing often. "Like I said before, I know I'm a scoundrel, and not just for the way I've treated Katie, even though that's been pretty bad and I'm terribly sorry. And I realize that there's nothing I could ever do to make up for that. But I do believe, Jesus, that you died for me and took the punishment I deserve. I receive you this moment as my Savior. Thank you for dying that horrible death for me."

After a long pause, he looked up into Katie's eyes. Lucas wasn't surprised to see tears on Katie's cheeks, but Katie was surprised to see her husband's eyes glisten.

For a while he just stared at his wife with a strange smile on his face. Then he gently pulled her close beside him. He took her in his arms and silently stroked her hair, holding her as if he'd never let go.

"Lucas," Katie finally said, afraid to speak, but still curious. "You said that two things became clear to you when you were upstairs earlier. The first was that you wanted to know God. What was the second?"

"Well, the second was that in spite of all my effort, you've won. I'm ready to admit my defeat. I can see now that I really never had a chance."

"What are you talking about? I haven't been fighting you, Lucas," Katie answered in confusion.

"Oh, yes you were," he replied firmly. Your aggression began the moment I stepped off the plane when I returned from Hawaii. You were battling for your husband's affections and you were successful. I've come to care for you more deeply that I thought was possible. I love you, Katie, so very much. Dare I hope you've been able to come to love me a little...even after I've told you the truth about myself?"

"No, Lucas," Katie replied quite seriously. When she saw concern wash over his face, she quickly finished with a sly smile. "Not a little...for I've loved you dearly for some time now. I'm overwhelmed that you finally return my love."

He kissed her in a way he'd never done before... a sweet tender kiss full of meaning. Then he held her close for a while longer as they watched the last embers of the fire grow dim. The loving closeness of her husband felt so unbelievably wonderful. Katie's heart overflowed with gratitude to a loving God. What a matchless Christmas gift!

Lucas released his embrace abruptly. "What time is it?" he said excitedly.

Katie looked at her watch and replied, "It's 8:45."

"Get your coat, Katie! If we hurry, we can still make it!"

"Make it to what? What are you talking about?" Katie was really puzzled.

"Why to church, of course. I saw on the sign in front of a little church a few miles from here that they were having a 9:00 P.M. Christmas Eve Service. At the time I thought that was the last place I'd want to be on Christmas Eve, but right now that sounds perfect!"

Katie shook her head in amazement as she hurried to her bedroom to repair the damage done by the earlier tears and distress of the evening.

By the time they drove up to the same little church Katie had attended before, the service had already begun. The room was dimly lit by well-placed crimson candles. A man whom Katie recognized to be the pastor was leading the small group in singing *Silent Night*. Katie was pleasantly surprised to hear the familiar words come in mellow tones from her husband's lips. When the song was finished, the children of the group were invited to sit around the Christmas tree at the front of the small auditorium while the pastor told the dear old story of Jesus' birth. As Katie sat pondering the wonder of Christmas, Lucas took her small hand into his. It was hard to comprehend the love in his eyes as he frequently glanced her way.

Then the service was over, and Katie found herself fearing she might wake up and find all this was only a wonderful dream. Lucas leaned over close and whispered, "Wait here just a minute." As the friendly church people came up to greet her, she lost sight of her husband. Just when his absence was beginning to make her nervous, he returned to her side. Everyone wanted to meet Katie's husband, so it was a while before they turned to move toward the door. Once again Lucas leaned over and whispered, "I have a surprise for you. I hope you like it."

"What is it?" she queried.

"You'll see very soon," was all he said.

When they were almost ready to leave, they came to the door of the pastor's study. Lucas took Katie by the elbow and guided her into the small library. The pastor had conveniently stepped out of the room, and Lucas closed the door.

When he turned to face her, she was suddenly nervous again. Lucas' expression was solemn. She couldn't imagine what this could mean. Her handsome husband just quietly stared at her until she felt like squirming. Finally she couldn't take it anymore.

"What is this all about, Lucas?"

"You really are beautiful, you know," he responded still not smiling.

"I am not," she sputtered, "And I'm sure that's not why you brought me in here."

"No, you really are lovely. I never let myself fully comprehend that these last months. I can't decide whether you are more attractive on the outside or on the inside."

He would have gone on, but Katie interrupted. "I appreciate the sweet compliments, but would you please tell me what is going on?" she said firmly.

Still very serious, he took both of her hands in his and said, "Katie, if you could please, just for a moment, try to forget the last eight months and give me an honest answer."

He waited for a nod from Katie then looked deep into her eyes and continued, "Katlyn Marie Lehman, I love you with all my being. Will you marry me…again?"

"You mean we're not really married? It wasn't legal?" Katie pulled away horrified.

"No, Silly," Lucas chuckled. "Let me start over. When I married you last May, it was for all the wrong reasons. Now I have the very best of reasons to have you as my wife, so I thought if you were, well…that is…I love you and I'm hoping, and now I'll be praying that you can forgive me and love me, too. And the friendly reverend out there said he'd be willing, if you were, to perform a little ceremony to repeat our wedding vows tonight. Then I could promise to love and honor you until death do us part and really mean it this time.

Suddenly he stopped, pulled her close, and kissed her gently. Before releasing his hold, he whispered close to her ear, "Please say, 'yes.'"

Katie needed no time to decide. "Yes," she said simply in a tone full of meaning.

"Yes?" Lucas sounded incredulous.

"Yes!" she answered, laughing softly.

In the soft candlelight beside the Christmas tree at the front of the little country church, Katie and Lucas pledged their love for each other. As the moments passed, Katie felt as if she were in a glorious dream. Yet the warm touch of her husband's hand gently squeezing hers was real. The touch of his lips to hers when the minister finally said with a smile, "You may kiss the bride," was also very real. Katie's heart swelled with joy as she recognized God's wondrous goodness and mercy in giving her more than she imagined possible.

EPILOGUE

It was the same great room. The huge Christmas tree stood in the same corner it had been in for the last seven Christmases. The carefully-crafted nativity set was once again in its place of honor on the mantle over the fireplace, but something about the room was so very different than it had been seven years before. There were many more brightly-wrapped presents under the tree. Pictures with smiling faces adorned the walls. A toy truck peaked out from under the couch and a soft baby doll dressed in pink sat prettily in the corner of the comfy rocking chair that had been added to the room.

The real difference was the playful atmosphere. Children's voices squealed in giggles as the tots picked up the couch pillows to do battle with the also laughing enemy.

"You can't get me, Daddy. I get you wif my piwwo!" the two year old tot with dark curly hair exclaimed.

Lucas pretended to retreat in fear as the six year old blond tornado joined the attack. "I'll save you, Evan! Just don't let him grab you!"

At that moment the big arms reached out and swept both screaming children off their feet and onto the carpeted floor, with the smaller boy on top of his older sister.

"Ha!" Lucas laughed in triumph. "I got two on a pile! I win!"

Immediately the calls for aid went out as they struggled to escape. "Mommy, help! Daddy's got us in a pile!"

They all watched the door to see if Mommy would come to the rescue, but instead, a round, almost bald, head appeared very close to the ground. Hands and knees moved quickly as he scurried toward the ruckus.

"No, Tommy! No!" the cry went out. "Daddy will get you! Go back! Don't come any closer!"

But it was too late. Lucas grabbed the new victim up and plopped him down on his brother's tummy.

"Daddy's the winner and still the champion!" Lucas said with a laugh as he released his hold on the squirming children.

Just then they all heard footsteps on the hardwood floor right outside the room. With a twinkle in his eye, the children's father whispered, "Let's get Mommy now. You kids pretend you're still in my trap and call Mommy to come help you. When she gets close, then Daddy will catch her."

Immediately the two older siblings hopped into Lucas' lap and began to exclaim in an exaggerated tone, "Mommy, Mommy, help us! Daddy's got us! Help! Help!"

The baby crawled a few feet away, sat up, and clapped his hands with glee as his mother entered the room with a smile.

"Help us, Mommy!" the older children continued between giggles.

As Katie leaned over to pull the children to safety, Lucas suddenly released his captives and grabbed his wife, pulling her down on his chest. At once he began to tickle his new prisoner mercilessly.

"Lucas, stop it! Stop…tickling…me," she choked out between uncontrollable laughter.

The handsome attacker hesitated thoughtfully. "Maybe you can buy your freedom," Lucas answered with a sly smile, still maintaining his firm hold on her.

"What's your price?" Katie questioned with obvious distrust.

Lucas tried to look serious as he replied, "Only a kiss from the pretty lady."

Immediately the watching youngsters chimed in, "Kiss him, Mommy! Kiss Daddy, and he'll let you go."

"All right," she answered mischievously, "If I *have* to."

Lucas pulled her close and accepted a brief but loving kiss.

As Katie stood to her feet she announced, "It's time for you munchkins to go to bed. The first one upstairs gets to pick out the Bible story for tonight!"

Immediately little feet began to scurry up the stairs as Katie picked up the baby.

After Katie had put her three to bed, she searched out her husband, finding him sitting on the couch in the great room with a fire blazing in the fireplace.

"Come here, Kitten," Lucas said when he saw her in the doorway. "Sit with me by the fire for a little while."

Katie snuggled up against him, silently watching the flames dance and listening to the quiet Christmas music playing in the room. After several minutes of holding her close, Lucas leaned over and whispered in her ear a soft, "thank you".

Katie looked up at him with a loving smile and quietly inquired, "Thank you for what, Luke?"

"For being you…for loving me…for letting me see Jesus in you in such a way that I wanted to know Him, too.

Printed in the United States
203166BV00001B/148-1023/P